Joseph Richardson

A Complete Investigation of Mr. Eden's Treaty

as it may affect the commerce, the revenue, or the general policy of Great Britain

Joseph Richardson

A Complete Investigation of Mr. Eden's Treaty
as it may affect the commerce, the revenue, or the general policy of Great Britain

ISBN/EAN: 9783337402396

Printed in Europe, USA, Canada, Australia, Japan

Cover: Foto ©Andreas Hilbeck / pixelio.de

More available books at **www.hansebooks.com**

A

COMPLETE INVESTIGATION

OF

JAEN's **TREATY,**

ᴀꜱ ɪᴛ ᴍᴀʏ ᴀꜰꜰᴇᴄᴛ

ᴍᴍᴇʀCE, THE REVENUE,

ᴏ ʀ

GENERAL POLICY

ᴏ ꜰ

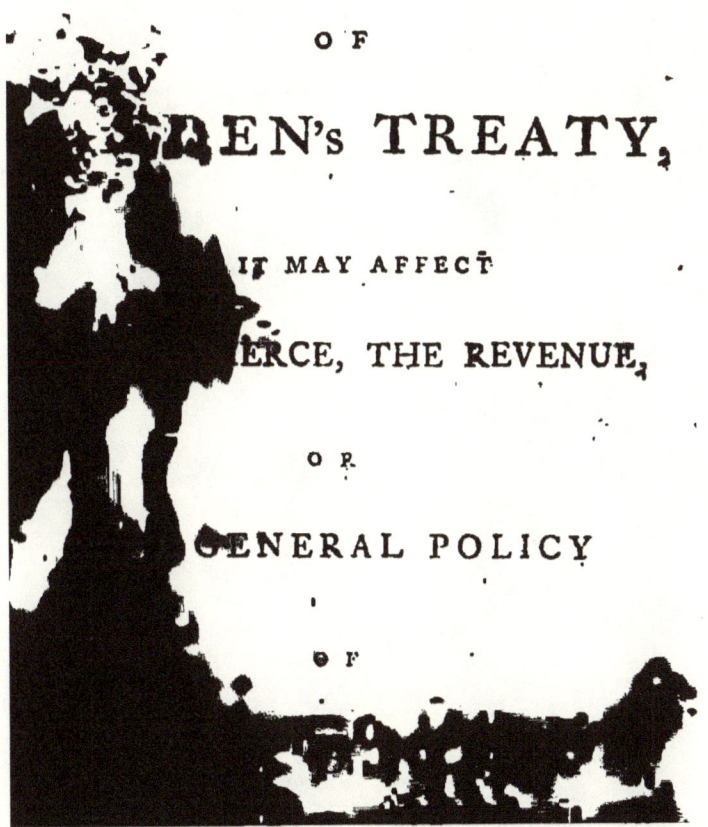

A

COMPLETE INVESTIGATION

O F

Mr. EDEN's TREATY.

THE Treaty, which it is the object of thefe Remarks fairly and candidly to difcufs, will be readily allowed by every perfon at all intelligent in the Commercial or Political Syftems of this country, to contain regulations at once new and important. Their novelty will be an excufe for a jealous, though impartial inveftigation; and the magnitude of their object will be a juftification for the minutenefs or elaboration of detail, in which an enquiry of this fort demands to be involved.

Som

Some of the oldeſt habits which have pre-. vailed in this country will receive a new di- rection by the operation of this Treaty; many of its uſeful ſuperſtitions will be ſhaken, and its moſt fixed principles ſubverted. It is not meant to be contended that the opi- nions of our anceſtors are infallible, or that innovation is always criminal : but this much will ſurely be acceded to us, That of all the ſubjects upon which the human judgement can poſſibly be exerciſed, there is none which ſo much demands that its principles ſhould be deduced from fact, and be ſanctioned by ex- perience (in caſes, that is to ſay, like the pre- ſent where fact and experience are practicable to be obtained) as commerce. It will at leaſt, therefore, be conſidered as a firſt preſump- tion againſt the wiſdom of a new ſcheme of commercial regulation, if it ſhould be found to militate not only againſt the traditional theories of our forefathers, for that would be of leſs conſequence, though not totally to be deſpiſed, but the ſettled habits of their prac- tice. It will be held perhaps to be ſomething more than a mere preſumption againſt the prudence of ſuch an innovation, if it ſhould further appear that upon the obſervance of that particular principle, which it immediately

tends

tends to deftroy, has uniformly depended the wealth, induftry, and commercial profperity of the country.

It will be the object therefore of a few of the enfuing pages to demonftrate this pofition from hiftory, That in the proportion as the trade between England and France has been. open or fhut, have the interefts of Englifh commerce flourifhed or declined.

It was not till the reign of the *Stuarts*, however unpropitious their principles threatened to be' to the political or conftitutional government of the country, that the commerce of England began to prevail to any confiderable degree;—it flourifhed under the difturbances of thefe turbulent times, becaufe in the midft of internal conflict and diforder, many falutary regulations were made refpecting it.—Amongft thefe, a free trade with France was certainly not of the number; on the contrary, the ports of both countries were mutually fhut to each other, and all commercial intercourfe was to the full as feverely interdicted as it remains at this day.

After

After the Reſtoration, when French manners, faſhions, and principles were introduced by Charles the Second, the idea of a trade with that country became the prevalent caprice of the day, and was encouraged with infinite zeal, by the profound aſſemblage of gay politicians that ſurrounded that prince. About the year 1675, however, the attention of the nation was ſeriouſly called to the ſtate of its commerce by a very remarkable circumſtance, which alarmed all the ſtateſmen in the country, and which is taken notice of by all the writers of that period, viz. a univerſal fall in the landed eſtates all over England. After an accurate inveſtigation into the cauſes of this event, one remarkable fact preſented itſelf to the obſervation of ſuch as had taken the pains of the enquiry, that the trade with France had grown to ſuch an extravagant extent in articles of mere luxury, and the balance of exports and imports ſo enormouſly againſt England, that the drain had become more than the nation was able to ſuſtain, and had proved the real ſource of the evil complained of, an evil which had not only operated a vaſt diminution of our commerce, but a moſt alarming danger to the more immediate and vital intereſt of the empire,

the

the Landed Property. Many able merchants
drew up a ftate of the trade between England
and France, as it ftood in the year 1674,
which is ftill to be found in the books of the
Cuftom-houfe, and which was prepared by
order of the Commiffioners for concluding a
Treaty of Commerce with France.

They ftate, that the value of all the goods exported to France from England amounted to	171,021	6	0
While the value of the imports from France amounted to the enormous fum of	1,136,150	4	0
Balance againft England - £.	965,128	18	0

Thefe Commiffioners, who appear to have
been men that underftood the nature of the
duty to which they had been delegated, and
were determined to execute, with virtue and
patriotifm, the objcct of an appointment
which they comprehended with perfpicuity
and precifion, conclude their report thus:

" By the above account, your Lordfhips
will perceive that the linen and filk manufactures only, imported from France, amount
to

to upwards of eight hundred thousand pounds; and the manufactures of wool and silk exported from England thither, do not amount to eighty-five thousand pounds.—As also all other commodities of the product and manufactures of England exported into France, do not amount to ninety thousand pounds more. Whereas the wines, brandies, and other commodities of the product and manufactures of France imported into England, amount to upwards of three hundred and twenty thousand pounds, besides an incredible value of toys, rich apparel, point lace, &c. So that it is apparent that the exports of our native commodities and manufactures to France, are less in value by at least one million of pounds sterling, than the native commodities and manufactures of France, which we receive from them."—*Com. Jour.* vol. 17, p. 423.

Notwithstanding, however, the above alarming representation, yet such was the King's determined partiality towards France, to use a phrase, certainly not the most descriptive of the fact, but the least offensive to the delicacy, which is by some conceived to belong to the discussion of the regal character, that a Treaty of Commerce was concluded between that

country

country and England, which fo far from turn-
ing out to the advantage of the latter, only
tended to increafe the evils already complained of. *Anderfon*, in his valuable Hiftory
of Commerce, ftates, that the balance againft
England in its trade with France, increafed
to the amount of 1,330,000l. exclufive of
600,000l. annually run, or fmuggled in upon
us.

Imports from France,	—	1,500,000
Exports,	—	—	170,000
		£. 1,330,000

" And thus," fays he, " all our grave laws
againft the exportation of fpecie, when the
balance of trade is againft us, is but hedging
in the cuckow."

Luckily for the pride of England, the parliament and the people did not entirely fym-
pathize in the devotion of their monarch. —
They had no motive for refifting the influence
of facts ;—they beheld with a natural alarm,
the dangers to which they were expofed, and
urged their fenfe of it with a commendable
vehemence;

vehemence; the voice of the multitude when exercifed on the fide of truth, is not to be oppofed for ever. Accordingly, in the enfuing year, after the ratification of the Treaty, namely in 1678, we find the Commons uniting in the general fenfe of the public. They came to a vote declaring, " the trade with France detrimental to the kingdom ;" and foon after an act was paffed, exprefsly prohibitory of the trade with France, to which was prefixed the following preamble:

" Forafmuch as it hath been by long experience found that the importing French wines, brandy, linen, filks, falts, and paper, and other commodities of the growth, product, or manufactures of the territories and dominions of the French king, hath much exhaufted the treafure of this nation, leffened the value of the native commodities, and manufactures thereof, and caufed great detriment to this kingdom in general."—

That this fpirited interpofition on the part of the parliament, fo directly in hoftility with all the views and wifhes of the court, was not made before the circumftances of the country made it indifpenfibly neceffary, is

is eafily deducible from the concurrent teftimony of all the co-temporary writers. I
fhall content myfelf with *Anderfon's* comment
upon this reprobated intercourfe with France,
who relates the refult of it in this fhort but
emphatical defcription :

" THE FOREIGN TRADE OF ENG-
" LAND LANGUISHED, AND THE
" RENTS FELL."

From the period of the prohibition, which
has been juft mentioned, our trade again revived, and that not by the flow operation of
time and gradual improvement, but rapidly
and at once. The balance became again in
our favour, and fo continued, with a triumphant
fuccefs, equally beneficial to the country, and
infulting to the corrupt inclinations of the
court, till the year 1685, the beginning of the
reign of James the IId. who again determined
to renew the whole train of experienced mifchiefs confequent on an open trade with France.
In this inaufpicious year, the prohibition of
1677 was repealed, and the commerce between the countries was again laid open.
It is not the purpofe of thefe Remarks to
comment upon the inducements which pre-

C   vailed

vailed with James the IId. to refume this
pernicious policy. It is fufficient to relate the
fact, and to repeat again the fame tale of an
inftantaneous influx of evils proceeding from
it. The meafure was no fooner adopted than
the French commerce advanced, as if by en-
chantment, to a magnitude fuperior even to
what it had ever attained at any other period
of fimilar indulgence. France had begun by
this time to be confcious of the advantages of
her own fituation, and of the immenfe obligations which fhe owed to nature. The minifter of Louis had not been inattentive to
the cultivation of them. This policy co-operated with the imprudence of the government
of this country, in making the laft advance
of her commerce not only fomewhat more
fudden, but more extenfive than any other
progreffion which it had ever before experienced. The very firft year after the trade
was opened, as appears by accounts laid before
the Houfe of Commons, the imports entered
at the Cuftom-houfe amounted to the enormous
fum of   -   -   £. 1,284,419 10   3
Goods clandeftinely import-

ed,   -   -   428,139 17   9
                                      ―――――――――――
                                      1,712,559   7   0

3   While

While the exports amount-
ed only to the fum of   515,228 14   3
                             ─────────────────
Lofs to England   -   1,197,330 12   9
                             ─────────────────

At a medium of three years, the importation
from France amounted to the fum of 1,460,000l.
exclufive of wine and brandy.   Fortunately,
for this country, as well for its commerce as
for its internal policy, this fatal fyftem ended
with all the other projects of James the IId.
and the fame year which reftored freedom.
to the conftitution by feating William the
III. upon the throne, gave new life to commerce by a renovation of the prohibitions
upon the import of French goods.   And
indeed moft highly neceffary had it become
that the old and beneficial fyftem of the
country fhould be reverted to, for our rivals
had fpared no exertion of art or induftry to
maintain that fuperiority which their climate,
the cheapnefs of their labour, and the plenty of
their raw materials gave them.   Councils of
Commerce, confifting of the moft experienced
traders, were formed in every part of France,
and every encouragement which experience
could fuggeft, or power could give effect to,

was prefented to the manufacturers. It is to thefe inftitutions co-operating with their na-·tural advantages, that one of our moft intelligent authors afcribes, " the almoft furprifing encreafe of the commerce, woollen manu-factures, mercantile fhipping, and foreign colonies of France."

The commerce between the two countries remained in this ftate of reciprocal prohibition till the year 1713, when in the adjuftment of a treaty of peace at Utrecht, conducted under the direction of that able minifter, Monf. *de Torcy*, a new attempt was made to introduce the favourite fyftem of France, an open trade with England. This experiment paffed upon the ignorance of the Englifh negociator, but was not equally fuccefsful with the parliament and the people.

The reader will not complain of the length of the above narrative, when he reflects upon the importance of its tendency. It proves beyond all power of contradiction, becaufe upon the bafis of actual hiftory, and the authority of official documents, the conftant alterna-tions of fuccefs or ruin to our commerce, as the trade of France was fhut or open. Till a better criterion can be inftituted for deter-mining

mining upon the probability of the *future*, than a reference to the *paft*, it will not be denied, that fome ufe is to be derived from fuch a review as that which has juft been taken.

In reply to this narrative, if it fhould be fuggefted, that the avenues to a reciprocal commerce between the two countries may be faid to have been opened by the treaty of Utrecht, which was never *in toto* annulled, let it be remembered that, though the whole of that treaty was never entirely abrogated, yet that the commercial part of it never had any exiftence at all.

That, the general body of the inhabitants of this country were content with the refufal given by the Houfe of Commons to the admiffion of the 8th and 9th articles of the treaty, and having triumphed in the rejection of the parts principally objectionable, were lefs anxious to purfue it, through its lefs offenfive detail.

That from the intervention of long and bitter hoftilities between the two countries, and by the neglect of the legiflature of Great Britain to pafs fuch laws as were neceffary for giving entire effect to feveral ftipulations of the treaty, it has been feldom acted upon, and in conduct often directly contravened.

Let

Let it be remembered alfo, that it is one thing to fuffer the dead letter of a treaty to remain, of which the country might avail itfelf in cafes of particular exigency, and another to revive its efficient operation, and to extend its fpirit.

But above all let it not be forgotten, that many of the points which will be found to contain the moft fubftantial grounds both of alarming novelty, and direct and evident injury in the prefent treaty, had no exiftence at all in its prefumed prototype, the treaty of Utrecht.*

That under the treaty of Utrecht there was a direct and exprefs prohibition by ftatute

---

* By the treaty of Utrecht the tariff of 1664 was to be eftablifhed as the tariff; payable upon Englifh goods going to France, except in fo far as related to certain goods which were to pay the tariff of 1699.

But when French goods came to this country, England was only obliged to repeal fuch prohibitions or high dutiesas were peculiarly laid upon French goods, pofterior to the year 1664.

Therefore all goods prohibited prior to that period, continued to be fo under the treaty of Utrecht.

France infifted, that a tariff fhould be made in England fimilar to that of 1664 in France, by which the duties

tute againſt the importation of French woollens into this country.

The

duties and prohibitions ſhould have been reciprocal in
the two countries. Lord Bolingbrooke treated the idea
of a reciprocal tariff with diſdain. Vide, Report of
the Committee of Secreſy, p. 27.

Woollen goods of all ſorts, harneſs and ſadlery, hardware, and cutlery are prohibited to be imported by acts
paſſed, 12th Edw. III.—4th Edw. IV.—1ſt Rich. III.—
5th Eliz.—1ſt Cha. I.—16th Cha. I.——All theſe muſt
be repealed under the preſent treaty, and would all have
continued in force under the treaty of Utrecht.

By the tariff 1664, theſe articles paid upon their entry
into France the following duties :

	Liv. S.
Hardware of copper, -	6 0 per Cwt.
Hardware of iron, -	1 12
All ſorts of cutlery, turnery, &c. comprehended in French under the name of mercerie, -	4 0
Sadlery and harneſs 5 per cent. ad valorem.	

The tariff 1664 in France was calculated upon a
principle of 5 per cent. being the amount of the duty
upon every article contained in it. Mr. Eden's tariff
is above double in every inſtance.

Even the excepted ſpecies, broad cloth, by the
tariff 1699, would have had to pay only 55 livres per
piece of 25 aunes in length by 5 quarters wide.—

The

That Englifh woollens might have been imported into Franceat a duty of 10$\frac{1}{2}$ per cent.

The French aune is 46$\frac{2}{7}$ inches Englifh, which makes the length of the piece 32 yards 3$\frac{4}{7}$ inches, and the breadth 57$\frac{3}{4}$.

This makes the piece equal nearly to a piece of Englifh broad cloth of 30$\frac{1}{2}$ yards long, which at 17s. a yard, is per piece 25l. 10s. 0d.

And valuing the livre at one fhilling, its value at the figning the treaty of Utrecht, the duty upon broad cloth would not have amounted to above 10$\frac{6}{8}$ per Cent.

As the French coin has undergone a variety of alterations, it may be for the information of the reader to fubjoin a ftate of its value at different periods.

	Liv.	S.
In the year 1668 the mark of filver was valued at	26	0
Colbert altered it to	28	0
In the year 1709 it was valued at	40	0
In September, 1713, it was again reduced to	28	0
Between September, 1713, and Auguft, 1715, the French coin changed its value eleven times, varying between 28 and 40 livres.		
In Jan. 1716 the value of the coin was fixed at	40	0
In the year 1730 the mark was valued at	49	0
At prefent it is valued at	48	9

Sir James Stewart informs us, that the mark is nearly equal to 40 of our fhillings.

	s.	d.
The livre was therefore, in the year 1668, worth of our money,	1	6$\frac{8}{11}$
Colbert altered its value to	1	5$\frac{3}{14}$
In the year 1709, and at the time of figning the treaty of Utrecht, 11th of April, 1713, it was worth	1	0

per cent. which is only $1\frac{1}{2}$ lefs than the duty under the prefent treaty, when the terms of the importation are reciprocal.

That the duty upon French Brandy was more than twelve times the amount of the internal duty then impofed upon our own Diftilleries, whereas it is now little more than in the proportion of three to one.

That the Rum trade from our Weft India iflands, which now produces a duty to this country of upwards of 400,000l. was then comparatively nothing, and prefented therefore neither a fource of effential defalcation to the revenue, nor of deep injury to individuals.

That French fubjects were not only not permitted by that treaty to convert themfelves into citizens of Britain by the mere act of paffage, and to come into a participation of all the privileges conferred by the fanction of chartered rights, but were exprefsly prohibited fo to do.

That the Hardware and Cutlery of France were pofitively prohibited coming into this country, while ours were importable there on a duty of one livre, 12 fous per cwt. whereas the prefent duty is 10 pounds *per cent. ad valorem,* even though the importation is mutual.

D   That

That Harnefs, and every article of Hofiery and Sadlery might have gone from England to France, paying only a duty of *5 per cent.* while their importation of fimilar articles ftood directly and pofitively forbidden with England.

That by the treaty of Utrecht, the French engaged to abolifh the farm of tobacco; or in other words, to give to our colonies the monopoly of their market; an immenfe advantage, for which, by this latter treaty, we have received no equivalent, nor feemed to expect a compenfation.

That by the former treaty, cottons might have been fent to this country, upon a duty of *5 per cent.* while it refted with us to put what duty we pleafed on the importation of French cottons; whereas the importation duty is now 12 *per cent. ad valorem*, and the right reciprocal. That neither the letter nor the fpirit of the Navigation act were at all infringed. And that the injurious diftinction in favour of France, known by the name of *Droit d'Aubaine*, was fpecifically and unambiguoufly abrogated. Such are the differences between the two treaties, and fuch the increafed motives for alarm that belong to that executed under the prudent aufpices of Mr. Eden.——

Eden. —— Under the circumſtances, then, which accompanied the original introduction of the treaty of Utrecht, and which have followed upon' it ſubſequently ·it will appear. That it can with no juſtice be conſidered· as containing any proof of the ſuſpenſion of that ſettled and preſcriptive abhorrence which the inhabitants of'this country have entertained with reſpect' to an open trade with France.—But if the inſtance were permitted to have an operation beyond what it can fairly claim, and what is only allowed it here for the ſake of argument, it could only' prove a diſpoſition on the part of the Engliſh for *ſuch a degree* of intercourſe with the French as was permitted under the terms of that treaty, and could with no propriety be adduced as a ſanction for the ſo much much more enlarged, expanded, *liberal* amity of communication, which is extended to them under the influence of Mr. Eden's new ſyſtem.

Was it weak ſuperſtition, or correct and well conſidered policy, that prevailed with our anceſtors in this unremitting diſlike to too near a contact with the French?

What anſwer can be given to ſuch a queſtion, but a reference to the events which have

D 2   taken

taken place under it.—The French have fought
for a century, with the exertion of every active
and infidious policy, to accomplifh this bro-
therly reciprocity of connection and friendfhip.
The year 1787 will be the firft period of their
enjoyment of it.—Have they been urging this
for fo long a fpace of time, and we declining
it, with a mutual ignorance on both parties,
they of their own good, and we of our own
danger ?—The fact is, nations feldom err long
in points that refpect their own immediate advantage. Cafual prejudice, or occafional incapacity in their rulers may miflead them
for a time; but the regular influence of
underftanding and intereft will prevail at
laft. That which has been anxioufly defired by one power, and as vehemently re-
fufed by the other, through a variety of changes of government and of circumftances,
which has been fteadily purfued by every
defcription of minifters in the one country, however repugnant in their general
politics—and as uniformly refifted by every
fucceffion of difagreeing politicians in the
other—is evidently to the advantage of the
power which feeks, and to the injury of that
which rejects : The uniform prevalence of
fuch a fentiment, is the demonftration of experience

perience delivered through the medium of the united fenfe of both empires; and, if any thing can decide upon the direction of their refpective interefts, this muft.

TARIFF.

I fhall proceed now to the confideration of that part of the treaty which is entirely commercial. The reader will be aware, that in the difcuffion of fuch a fubject, a good deal of detail is neceffary and unavoidable. No ftatement will be obtruded upon him here, which can be done without; but many it will be my indifpenfible duty to fubmit to him. Without thefe, he can neither know with any precifion the extent and nature of the advantages which this country is reprefented as being likely to obtain from the prefent treaty, nor the degree of expence fhe is to pay for them, if obtained at all.

One obvious idea muft prefent itfelf to the moft carelefs obferver on this department of the fubject, namely, that the Four firft articles of the tariff contain ftipulations in favour of France, for which the moft remote appearance of a reciprocal advantage is not fo much as pretended. They ftipulate in thefe articles to referve to
themfelves

themfelves the poffeffion of our market for their Wines, their Brandies, their Vinegars, and their oils, which are all the ftaple produce of their own country, and in which, fo far from having an equivalent advantage, we cannot have the moft diftant degree of competition. It would have been natural, in fuch a fituation, for the minifter of this country to have infifted upon fome fpecific return, fome permanent benefit, in compenfation for fuch extraordinary conceffions. The pretended principle of the treaty is reciprocity—how then is it, that, in the very commencement of it, we fee no lefs than four diftinct and capital advantages conferred, for which not only not an adequate return is made, but no return at all ?

But it will be faid, perhaps, the counterbalance to thefe advantages is received by us in the remaining part of the Tariff.—No fuch thing. —In every other part,—the Cottons, the Woollens, and every other article of trade, permitted by the treaty to be reciprocally imported, have the market of England opened to them upon the fame terms on which the market of France is opened to the correfponding articles in England.—The fuperior benefit to either country, therefore, in thefe points, muft depend

depend folely upon the advantages of their internal fituation—fuch as cheapnefs of labour, cheapnefs of living, comparative exemption from taxes, &c.

With refpect to thefe Four firft articles, however, this is by no means the cafe.— They not only contain advantages for which no equivalent has been granted, but which are, in their nature, certain and permanent. An increafe of induftry on the part of the French, their cheaper labour; combining with a frefh addition of burthen on the part of the Englifh, or with other cafualties which it is impóffible to forefee, and which in all ages of the world have made manufactures and commerce fhift from one country to another, may, in a few years, deprive England of every pretence to fuperiority, which the fanguine and the partial are fo fond of imputing to her now.—Other nations may rival her in the French market, and the French may rival her in her own.— But the advantages granted to France in her wines, brandies, and oils, are in their nature expofed to no inftability either of caprice or competition :—they are the native produce of their land—they demand no fkill in preparing

—and

—and it is not therefore within the reach of accident to deprive her of them.

Is it to be mentioned as an excuse for these concessions in favour of France, that we have no article of native produce which we could have sent into France, in return for those of a similar nature sent here ? This indeed is a fact; but it is no justification for the nego-ciator of the peace, because the reciprocity might have been obtained in another way.— He might have demanded some advantages to be extended to some particular branch of our manufactures.—He might have stipulated that our Hardware, or our Woollen, should have gone into their market at such a comparative inferiority of duty, as might have been thought sufficient to cover the advantage gained by the encouragement given to her wines and brandies; and have made the general principle, at least, if not the operation of the compact, reciprocal.

No man treated the pretended reciprocity of the Irish Propositions with more ridicule than Mr. Eden. When the Minister proposed that English Linens should be admitted into Ireland upon the same duty on which Irish Linens were admit-ted into England, and that the Woollens of both countries should stand precisely upon the same footing,

footing, the Negociator was loud in his reprobation of such a doctrine of Reciprocity.—
England neither does nor can manufacture Linen
in any degree of comparison with the Irish linens
—Ireland can and does manufacture Woollens.
It was therefore a Mockery of England to tell
her, that she might carry her Linens (*which she
could not make*) to Ireland free from duty,
because the Irish imported their's on the same
terms into England—but that Woollen, which
England *can* manufacture, should be subject to
a duty of 10 ½ *l. per cent.* because the Woollens
of Ireland (which Ireland can also manufacture) were exposed to a like duty in England.

Mr. Eden contended, and contended unan-
swerably, that the only possible idea of equitable Reciprocity was this—that as England admitted the staple of Ireland free from duty,
Ireland should admit the Staple of England
upon the same terms.—What a misfortune it
is that the Negociator had not recollected his
own reasoning, in a case where the application
of it was so much stronger, and the necessity
for the use of it so much more pressing than in
the instance of Ireland!—The staple produc-
tions of France are in future to be admitted into England, upon duties which will effectually

E   secure

secure to her, the monopoly of our market :— for a counterbalance to which advantage, so extensive in its effect, so permanent in its duration, no one benefit of any kind is stipulated in favour of England.

But these indulgencies to France are not only to be censured in as much as they want fairness, or even as they affect the Revenue—there is another point of view in which they will appear to be equally reprehensible.—The policy which has hitherto directed the Councils of this country, with regard to such articles of consumption as could not be produced at home, has been either to encourage the consumption of similar articles of her colonial produce, (as rum, in preference to Brandy) or to encourage the consumption of the articles in question, from that country, which, in return, either afforded us a Vent for our manufactured produce, or supplied us with Raw materials, for the employment of our internal industry.

It was upon this principle, that the duty has been kept high on French brandy and French wines.—It was upon this principle, that it was low upon the wines of Spain and Portugal.—These two countries afford the principal mar-

ket

ket for our woollens, and the produce of our
Newfoundland fishery; and, in return, they
send us Wool, Cotton, Cochineal, Indigo, Barilla, and Dying Drugs.

In every national confideration, except partiality of tafte, it is indifferent whether the
wines of France, or of Spain or Portugal, be
confumed in England.—But, if the Spaniard
or Portuguefe, in return for the preference
given to his wine, takes his cloth from our manufacturer, and his food from our fisheries—if
he fends us thofe articles without which our
manufactures cannot fubfift, and raw materials
for the exercife of our national induftry—there
becomes a motive of found and judicious policy for giving him our market, and for facri-
ficing an unimportant preference of tafte, to
the fubftantial confideration of a great public
advantage.

To have a clear and comprehenfive underftanding, therefore, of all the confequences
which may refult from the indulgencies extended to France in the four firft articles of the tariff, it will be neceffary to take a review of the
trade of this country with Portugal and Spain;
and to examine, how far the Revenue, Com-

merce,

merce, or Policy of England, will be affected by the changes introduced into it by the new arrangement.

THE TRADE WITH PORTUGAL.

WINES,

The obvious and necessary effect of reducing the duty upon French wines, must be the entire loss of the high duty upon all that quantity which is at present imported into this country. The quantity of French wine imported, upon an average of the four last years, as appears by an account laid before parliament by Mr. Pitt, on the introduction of his wine bill, amounts to 400 tons annually,

The present French duty is 96 *l.* 4 *s.* 1 *d.* which by the treaty is to be reduced to the duty now existing upon the wines of Portugal, that is, to 45 *l.* 19 *s.* 2 *d.*—or, in other words, the present French duty is to be lowered precisely 50 *l.* 4 *s.* 11 *d.* *per* ton.

This sum, multiplied by the average quantity imported, will yield no less an amount than 20,098 *l.* 6 *s.* 8 *d.* loss of revenue, which

I   is

is the first defalcation fustained by it under the operation of this treaty.

In every possible event this sum must be lost to the public, and will demand in some manner to be made good to the revenue.

If the quantity consumed of the respective wines of each country should remain precisely the same, then it is demonstrative, that the difference between the former and future duty upon the present quantity of French wines, 50l. 4s. 11d. per ton, upon four hundred tons, is entirely lost.

If, as is evidently intended by the Treaty, the quantity of French wine consumed here be encreased, still, as it will in future pay only the Portugal duty, the same sum is equally defalcated from the revenue.—In every alternative, therefore, this sum is gone.

But by the eighth article of the treaty, England reserves a power in favour of Portugal, of lowering the duty upon her wines to the proportion settled by the *Metheun* treaty; that is, to two thirds of that upon the wines of France, whatever it may be. If this power should

fhould not be exercifed, it is eafy to perceive
England muft relinquifh all hope of a commercial intercourfe with Portugal. The fuperior pleafantnefs and lightnefs of the French
wines, the lownefs of the freight, and, in
many inftances, the cheapnefs of the prime coft
of the article itfelf, will foon give a decided
preference to the wines of France. In this
event, the revenue would be a lofer to no
greater extent than has been already mentioned. But the effects to the trade of the
country would be truly alarming. We muft
prepare ourfelves to expect prohibitions in
Portugal upon the importation of our woollens, and the produce of our fifheries, and for
the various other confequences of fo important
a revolution, which, though equally certain,
are not with equal facility to be afcertained.

If, upon the other hand, this power fhould
be exercifed, and the referved right of diminifhed duty upon Portugal wines fhould be
actually carried into effect, then a new confequence arifes to the revenue. This, indeed,
muft vary in the proportion of the quantity of
Portugal wine which fhall continue to be confumed in England. It is impoffible to determine

mine at present, what the future changes in that confumption may be. We know, however, what it is at this time, and upon the fuppofition that it fhould remain the fame, the following will be the lofs to the revenue.

The prefent duty upon the wines of Portugal is 45l. 19s. 2d. per ton. One-third of this, which, by the Methuen treaty, is the ftipulated reduction below the French duty, is 15l. 6s. 4d. per ton.

The quantity of Port wine imported, amounted, upon an average of the four laft years, when the importation was rather falling off than otherwife, to 16,538 tons annually.

This number of tons, multiplied by the fum reduced upon each ton, that is, by 15l. 6s. 4d. will leave an amount of precifely 161,404l. 18s. 2d. which, added to the 20,098l. 6s. 8d. above-mentioned, makes the whole lofs to the revenue upon this article of 181,503l. 4s. 10d.

It is hardly poffible to fuppofe, under the prefent circumftances of the country, that it can be deliberately the intention of the minifter

mister to reduce the annual quantum of the
public purse by such an immense sum as the
above, the more so, when it is considered,
that it arises from an article which is, of all
others, the most proper object of taxation,
mere luxury. It is in candour, therefore,
to be presumed, that the intended effects
which are wished by the minister to be produced by the operation of the treaty, are the
encouraging the consumption of French wines,
and the producing a consequent diminution of
the consumption of those of Portugal.

A variety of circumstances concur to make
this latter supposition extremely probable.

The consumption of Portugal wines has
been encouraged in this country by a much
greater difference of duty than we were bound
by treaty to grant them; for though the stipulated difference of duty between the French
and Portugal wines is only one-third, yet in
point of actual practice, the duty of the
former has always been nearly double that
of the latter. For example, in 1763, when
the duty upon French wines was 66l. per
ton, the duty upon Portugal wine might

under

under, the terms of the treaty, have stood at
44l. per ton, yet it was in fact only 29l. and
in later years, when the French duty was
96l. 4s. 1d. the duty upon Portugal wines,
which might have been as high as 64l. per
ton, was no more than 45l. 19s. 2d. This
proportion of difference has continued since
the beginning of the century, and could not
but have a most powerful effect in encouraging the consumption of Portugal wines.—
How far a consumption which required to be
kept up by such a difference of duty as 50l.
per ton, will be protected by a difference only
of 15l. 6s. 4d. is not easy to conceive. If it
should be concluded, which may be done
under the *terms* of the present treaty, that
what has been practised under the *Methuen*
treaty may still continue to prevail, and that
the Portugal duties may be still diminished in
the old proportion with respect to the wines of
France, then let us see what will be the effect
in that view of the subject to the Revenue.
The future duty upon French wines is to be
45l. 19s. 2d. If the Portugal duties are to be regulated in the former proportion, that is, that
they may be something short of being half,
or, in other words, that they may be one-

F   third,

third, and one-sixth, instead of being two-thirds of the French duty, then it will be fair to estimate the future duty upon Port at about 22l. per ton. This will evidently make a defalcation of one-sixth of the whole duty upon Portugal wine more to the revenue than was estimated in the former instance, (for then the defalcation was calculated on a reduction of one-third, and is now reckoned on the supposition of its being diminished one-sixth more) which will amount, upon the whole annual importation of Port wines, to the sum of 80,702l. 9s. 1d. and must be added to the other two sums I have already mentioned, to make up the whole of the annual loss sustained to the public by the operation of the treaty.

There are a great variety of pleasant and strong wines from the South of France, which have been hitherto prevented from making their way into England by the enormous duty which has been indiscriminately laid upon all the wines of that country. When 15l. per ton becomes the only difference of duty, will there not be great reason to expect, that they may be had in England much cheaper than the wines of Portugal?

3

Very

Very excellent Languedoc wine, of a strength nearly equal to Port, and of infinite variety in its colour and flavour, may be purchased upon the spot at 14l. per ton.

The prime cost of a pipe of Port is about 17l. or 34l. per ton.

If we add the proposed duties to these, the former will still be considerably cheaper than the latter.

	l.	s.	d.
New French duty	45	19	2
Prime cost per ton	14	0	0
	59	19	2
New Portugal duty	30	12	10
Prime cost per ton	34	0	0
	64	12	10
	59	19	2

Difference of price altogether - - 4 13 8

To which is still farther to be added, the difference of freight and insurance between Oporto and Bourdeaux, which is considerable.*

* The French are also improving their advantages, by abolishing certain internal duties, which their wines have hitherto paid.

It may however be argued, and has, indeed, been strongly asserted, that the taste of this country is so decidedly in favour of Port wine, that even the difference of eighteen-pence on the duty will be quite sufficient to continue the importation of it in quantities nearly equal to what prevail at present.

This reasoning necessarily admits a defalcation of the revenue, or a loss of duty to the utmost extent of what has been above stated; *i. e.* of one-third of the present duty upon the whole quantity at present imported, together with the loss upon the French duty; to the amount of 181,503l. *per annum.* But the principle is certainly contradictory, both to the supposition of the treaty itself, and also to such facts as history furnishes us with upon the subject.

The treaty clearly supposes the diminution of the duty upon the wines to be an advantage to France, by increasing their exportation of that article, It would have been idle in *Her* to have asked in *Us*, and us to have granted, a reduction of duty, if her exportations were not chequed by the high duty at present subsisting upon them. As, however, our demand for wine is at present fully supplied, it is

clear,

clear, that whatever increased quantity of wine
we in future take from France, exactly in that
proportion must we diminish our imports of the
same commodities from other countries.

The ground and basis, therefore, of the
treaty is, that the French wine trade must en-
crease, and that of Portugal undergo a propor-
tionable diminution.

I am enabled by a resort to history to form
a very tolerable estimate of the degree of
reliance there is to be placed upon a supposed
preference of national taste in this country in
Favour of the wines of Portugal.

The Journals of the House of Commons
furnish us with an account of the importations of wine as they have stood at different
periods, when the trade was open, when it
was absolutely prohibited, or when it was
loaded with high duties; and from them it is
demonstrable, that national taste changed
exactly in the proportion as the commodity
was dear or cheap.

Tons

From the year 1675 to the year 1678, the
trade with France was open, and the importation of French wine, on an average,
was 8535

During

During the same period, the average importation of Portugal wine was
From the year 1679 to the year 1685 inclusive, the trade with France was prohibited, and the annual importation of Portugal wine was . . . 6880
From the year 1686 till the year 1695 inclusive, the trade with France was open, and the importation of French wine amounted annually to . . . 13401
During the same period, the importation of Portugal wine amounted, on an average, to . . . 488

And upon the trade with France being again, in King William's time, laid under prohibitory duties, the importation of French wine decreased to nearly the same quantity that has been, and is now annually imported.*

* Account of French and Portugal Wines imported during the first period.		Some account during the second period.		Some account during the third period.	
Fr. tons.	Port. tons.	Fr. tons.	Port. tons.	Fr. tons.	Port. tons.
1675 7495	20	1679 3	1013	1686 12670	286
1676 9645	83	1680 1	1003	1687 15518	327
1677 6289	176	1681 —	1718	1688 14218	448
1678 7212	199	1682 —	13860	1689 11109	579
		1683 —	16772		
34142	573	1684 —	11611	53605	1735
		1685 —	12885		
		4	55862		

From these facts, joined to the supposition admitted and justified by the article of the treaty itself, I am led to concur in the opinion which evidently prevailed with the negociators of it, that the lowering the duties on Portugal wine one-third, will not prove, in any degree, a protection to the importers of them.

This, then, is the situation in which we stand, with respect to Portugal.—If the comparative consumption of the wines of that country and France remain exactly the same in Great Britain as it stands at present, the revenue will be injured, to the amount of nearly 200,000l. *per annum.*

If, as is the much more probable alternative, the wines of France in their state of reduced duty, should drive the inferior ones of Portugal out of our market, the consequence will be the loss of the Portugal trade.

To this view of the subject I shall now proceed, and state such facts as may convince the public of its importance, and satisfy them how much we put to hazard by the probable effects of this indulgence to France.

The

The trade to Portugal has varied at different times, either as the Portuguese succeeded in the encouragement of their own manufactures, or as we have been rivaled in their market by other nations. It confifts principally at prefent in the exports of woollens, falt fifh, toys, watches, and other articles of luxury and convenience; to thefe were formerly added, confiderable quantities of hardware; but this laft article has of late much fallen off, owing to our being underfold in the Portugal market by the Flemifh manufacture of that article. This fact, which in a great meafure accounts for the fuppofed decay of the Portugal trade, was diftinctly in evidence before the Houfe of Lords, by the oaths of feveral of the principal manufacturers, and particularly by that of the intelligent *Mr. Gibbons.*

The export to that country is ftill of magnitude fufficient to awaken the fears of every well-wifher to his country, under the cafualty of its lofs.

By the accounts of the Infpectors' Books the export of Great Britain to Portugal is now higher than it has been for
some

It amounted in the year 1785 to a sum than 796,225l. of which, by much, the greater part was woollens.

But the inspectors' books furnish a much more fallacious account of the Portugal trade at present than they formerly did, when it is supposed to have been much higher than it now is.

Formerly the export to Portugal was principally carried on from the port of London; but the high port duties upon wine, and the high fees of every sort payable there, together with the circumstance of the woollen manufacture changing its situation, and settling principally in Yorkshire, has made the ports of Liverpool and Hull equal to that of London in this trade. However accurate the account of exports and imports from the port of London may be, nothing can be less so than the account which is kept at the out ports, where all the articles are thrown together, without care or accuracy, into one general head. Thus, while the inspectors' books state little more than 100,000l. as the account of our export to Portugal from all the out

ports,

ports, it is a notorious fact, that the town of Wakefield alone, sends woollens to the amount of double the sum; and that from eight to ten ships are cleared out from the port of Hull annually, which may be fairly reckoned worth from thirty to forty thousand pounds each.—— From these considerations it is apparent, that the Portugal trade is of infinitely more importance than is generally believed, and that the conceived decline of it arises only from the accident of its having changed its locality from the port of London to the out ports, where, as I have said, the accounts are kept with much less precision and distinctness.

But even these facts will not show the full extent of the benefit of the Portugal trade. If any article of export can be more beneficial to Britain than the export of her staple, an article of the trade to Portugal, which appears in no custom-house account whatsoever, is that one. I mean the produce of the fishery, which is carried on directly from Newfoundland to Portugal, and is to be found in none of the estimates of our exports and imports.

To

To thofe who are not accuftomed to confider the infinite importance of our fisheries, the extent of this article muft appear enormous, no lefs than 600,000 quintals of fish were, in the year 1784, fent in British veffels to foreign ftates from Newfoundland; and of this quantity about one-third went to Portugal.

An account of the price of a quintal of fish at Lifbon.

	s.	d.
Prime coft at Newfoundland -	10	0
Freight - - -	5	0
Infurance on coft, and freight at 3 per cent. - - -	0	5
Duty - - -	3	9
Commiffion and charges -	1	0
	£ 1	0 2

Of this fum the whole is paid to British fubjects, excepting only the fingle article of port duty. The prime coft and freight are the prices of the labour of our fishermen and failors, and the commiffion and charges are paid to British factors at Lifbon. The port duty, therefore, being deducted from the ac-

count,

count, will leave a sum of 16 s. 5 d. which multiplied by the number of quintals, will make the whole amount of the produce of the fishery sold to Portugal, 164,066 l. 13 s. 6 d. which, in considering the extent of the trade of that country, is to be added to every official representation derived from custom-house estimates.

With the addition, therefore, of this last branch of lucrative intercourse with Portugal, the whole value of our exports cannot, with any propriety, be estimated at less than 1,200,000 l. *per annum*; while our imports from thence have rarely amounted, in the same time, to above 350,000 l. which leaves a balance of trade in our favour of 850,000 l. *per annum*, arising from the export of goods which afford encouragement to our staple manufacture, and supplies a most powerful accession to the strength of our marine.

Except Wine, the only considerable article of our imports from Portugal is Cotton Wool, of a quality infinitely superior to that of any other part of the world. Of this we last year imported two millions of pounds.

It

TARIFF.

It is impossible to expect that when, by the operation of the French treaty, the Wines of France assume the place of those of Portugal in the consumption of Britain, the Portuguese will continue to take from us any articles of our manufacture. French Woollens till lately laid under prohibitory duties. Will she not have grounds for doing the same by those of Britain?

By the wisdom of the late treaty of peace, which extended the fishery of France in Newfoundland, Portugal can be at no loss to supply herself with that necessary article, should she lay high duties upon the English trade; and every interest she has to indicate the least preference to this country is at an end, the moment we have ceased to reciprocate benefits, by the rejection of her wines.

It is demonstrative, therefore, that this is the choice of evils, in this case, out of which the minister is compelled to make his selection— He must either relinquish a revenue to the amount of 200,000 *l. per annum*, or place in the utmost hazard, if not inevitable certainty of destruction, a branch of annual export, to the amount of 1,200,000 *l.* in order to preserve the revenue.

BRANDY.

BRANDY.

We fhall proceed now to another article of the tariff, upon which fuch a reduction of duty is ftipulated to be made in favour of France, as cannot fail, in its firft and certain operation, moft effentially to affect the revenue ; and, by its confequences, to produce a moft alarming injury, not only to a very valuable and exten- five part of our colonial trade, but even (by the mifchief which it muft extend to a moft productive branch of internal manufacture) prove, in the end, in the higheft degree injuri- ous to the agriculture and Landed Intereft of the Country.

The brandies of France, inftead of nine fhil- lings and fixpence $\frac{12}{20}$, are in future to pay no more than feven fhillings *per* gallon. Since the operation of the act of the twenty-fecond of his prefent Majefty, which equalized the cuf- tom duty upon all foreign brandies, little elfe than French brandy has been imported into this country. The fuperior quality, indeed, of the article itfelf, as well as the comparative advantage in the low price of freight from France, over any other competitor, would have

given

given to that country, the exclusive monopoly of the Britiſh market for her brandies, if no new encouragement had been extended to her by the operation of the preſent treaty*.

The quantity of brandy, upon an average of the two laſt years, which was imported and paid duty, amounted to 2857 tons, three hogſ-heads, two gallons—or 727,615 gallons.— Two ſhillings and ſixpence, the ſum taken from the preſent duty upon this quantity, will produce an immediate diminution of revenue to the amount of 90,981 *l.* 8 *s.* 6 *d.*

This loſs of duty, it is very evident, can on-ly be made good to the revenue by an immenſe encreaſe of the annual conſumption of bran-dy, or by the impoſition of a new tax upon ſome other article.

The quantity of brandy conſumed in this country cannot be increaſed, without a conſe-quent diminution in the conſumption of rum and home-made ſpirits, or an immoderate in-creaſe in the uſe of ſpirituous liquors—an evil

---

* The Miniſter was ſo ſenſible of this, that when he, two years ago, lowered the duties upon rum, he left the high duties upon brandy.

which

which it has been, and ever muſt be, the con-
ſtant object of a wiſe and virtuous legiſlature
to prevent.

We will not ſuppoſe that the miniſters of
this country mean to make good the loſs of
revenue by the corruption of morals ; or that
theymean to bring back again thoſe times, when
the legiſlature found it neceſſary to declare, as
in the preamble to the act known by the name of
the Gin Act, " That it was of the utmoſt im-
" portance to the public welfare, that ſome
" timely proviſion ſhould be made for prevent-
" ing thoſe miſchiefs, which muſt unavoidably
" enſue, ſhould ſpirituous liquors be again ſuf-
" fered to be ſold at a low rate."

If, therefore, the total quantity of ſpirits
conſumed in the country is not intended to be
increaſed, any increaſe on the conſumption of
brandy muſt affect that of rum and home-made
ſpirits, unleſs an equivalent diminution of duty
takes place upon them.   The miniſter, indeed,
appears to have had this in his contemplation,
and ſeems to think it a neceſſary and indiſpen-
ſible policy, that the lowering the duty upon

2   brandy

brandy should be secured against producing a consequent diminution in the use of rum. He has already hinted an inclination to lower the duty upon rum 3 *d. per* gallon.

The only principle upon which this decrease can be founded, is a wish to preserve a relative proportion in the consumption of each article. If this be done, the amount of the diminished rum duty must be added to the amount of the stipulated diminution of that upon brandy, as a certain and further degree of injury, to which the public purse is wantonly exposed.

The quantity of rum imported into this kingdom, on an average of four years preceding the year 1777, was 2,375,176 gallons. During the same period the export was 655,291 gallons. And the whole average annual consumption was 1,719,785 gallons.

I have chosen to select these years, because in them the importations were moderate. If I had been influenced by any disposition towards an uncandid advantage, I might have taken the year 1785, when the total importation amounted to 3,614,114 gallons; a quantity, as is very

H   apparent,

apparent, infinitely greater; but, perhaps, partly to be accounted for by caufes not permanent in their effect, and which, therefore, may not exift equally at another period.

Now threepence *per* gallon on 1,719,785 gallons, will produce a fum of 21,495*l.* 19*s.* 3*d.* Such is the amount of the reduced rum duty, which the minifter has even intimated his confent to make, in addition to what he has already given up upon brandy. But the Weft India planter neither is, nor can be, fatisfied or fecure, under this diminution. It is not fuch as will fecure him againft the increafed importation of brandy, which, even under the higher duties, he found every difficulty to ftruggle with.

The late war having fallen fo heavily upon the Weft Indies, having increafed the price of every thing in Britain with which they are fupplied, having loaded them with internal taxes in their iflands, having increafed both the price and the difficulty of procuring lumber from America, joined to the high freights and heavy infurances which they are obliged to pay, has fo confiderably raifed the price of their commodity,

modity of late years, that it is quite impoffible that 3 d. *per* gallon can bring the planter on a footing with the importer of French brandy.

The Weft India merchants, with a moderation which does them honour, have only foli-cited a reduction of 5 d. *per* gallon, which, upon the quantity already ftated, will amount to 35,826 *l.* 12 *s.* 1 *d.*

DISTILLERY.

But it is not only the Weft India planter who will be materially affected by the diminution of the duty upon brandy.

The MALT DISTILLERY will be equally hurt. It is a fact perfectly well known, that this branch of manufacture, fo valuable to the landed intereft of this country, is already in an alarming ftate of decline. It has confumed, in years paft, no lefs than 500,000 quarters of malted corn. Upon an average of the three years preceding 1782, it confumed fcarcely 200,000 quarters. It would be prefuming too much upon a fuppofed ignorance in the reader, to point out the immenfe advantage it is to the farmer to have such a market for his grain, or to the revenue, by what it pays in its progreffion of different stages from barley to spirits.

There was charged with duty, on an average of three years preceding 1782, 2,351,534 gallons of Britifh spirits. During that period, however, as the duty was laid upon the wafh by a conjectural calculation, which fuppofed that 100 gallons of wafh produced 15 gallons of spirit; and as that calculation has been fince found to be erroneous, and, by an act paffed in the year 1784, the 100 gallons of wafh are charged with duty upon a fuppofition of producing 20 gallons of spirit, we muft add the difference, to difcover the quantity really made.

The effect of the regulation in 1784 was that of increafing the number of gallons of spirits, charged with duty, one third. To the amount, therefore, of the average quantity upon which duty was charged the three years preceding 1782, muft be added one third, which will leave the given number of gallons that would be charged with duty from the

fame

fame quantity of wafh at this time. The third of 2,351,534 is 783,844. The two fums added, produce 3,135,378 gallons, which is the precife number upon which duty would now be charged.

The duty upon Britifh fpirits is now 2*s*. 6*d*. *per* gallon, calculating 100 gallons of wafh to produce 20 of fpirits. If it fhould be at all intended to fave this ufeful manufacture, the duties upon it ought, and muft be lowered, in the fame proportion as thofe of rum. If rum be lowered 5 *d. per* gallon, a proportionate reduction of the duty upon Britifh fpirits will amount to 2 *d. per* gallon—and this fum will amount, upon the quantity of fpirits above ftated, to 26,128 *l*. 3 *s. per annum*.

If this reduction of duty fhould not take place, it is not only the duty upon fpirits which will be deftroyed by the ruin of the diftillery, but the duty upon malt, which upon the quantity ufed in the diftillery amounts to above 100,000 *l*. will fuffer a proportional defalcation —the farmer will alfo lofe his beft market for his grain—fo that even the revered intereft of the landed property is to be, in fome degree,

3 among

among the facrifices which are to be made, for the encouragement of French induftry, and the confumption of French luxuries.

The above reafoning proceeds upon the fup-pofition, that the confumption of the feveral ar-ticles of fpirits, home and foreign, is to re-main, after the operation of the prefent treaty, precifely what it is at this time; and in that cafe the following defalcation will be fuftained by the revenue, namely,

Upon brandy	——	£ 90,951	8 6
Upon rum	——	35,826	12 1
Upon fpirits	——	26,128	8 0
Total defalcation on fpirits		152,906	8 7

If it fhould be contended, however, that this decreafe of duty upon the articles will be made up by a proportionate increafe upon their con-fumption, let us examine, what the degree of that increafe, upon fuch view of the fubject, muft neceffarily be. Upon calculation it will be found to ftand thus:

Of

TARIFF.	DISTILLERY.
Of brandy there muſt be increaſed in the conſumption	Gallons.
	259,860
Of rum ditto	153,522
Of home-made ſpirits	223,956
Total increaſe of conſumption to make up deficiency of revenue	637,338

Theſe then are the miſerable alternatives to which the people of Great Britain are to be re-duced. They are to ſubmit, in the article of ſpirits alone, to a reduction of the national re-venue to the amount of above 150,000 l. which by ſome expedient or other muſt be made good by new taxes—for the public creditor, it is preſumed, is not intended to be defrauded—or elſe their morals are to be corrupted, their health impaired, and their induſtry relaxed, by the increaſed uſe of a miſchievous luxury, the greateſt part of which is produced in another, and that a rival country.

COUNTERVAILING DUTIÉS.

All the articles of the tariff, except the four firſt, are founded at leaſt upon an of-tenſible

tenfible pretence to reciprocity. They prefume, that whatever may be the relative ftate
of fkill, taxation, or the price of labour, the
duties from ten to fifteen per Cent. are quite
fufficient to protect the manufactures of either
country, againft the competition of the other.

It is not however, a little remarkable, that
while the Irifh propofitions were in agitation,
the protecting duties being in that arrangement nearly upon an equivalent with thofe
of the prefent treaty, the manufacturers were
then unanimoufly of opinion, that fuch duties were perfectly inadequate to protect them
againft the manufacturers of Ireland?

If they were really fo in that cafe, may
it not be afked, how it happens that they
can be adequate to fuch a protection now,
when the *ad valorem* duty is fo little higher,
and the danger of the rivalfhip fo much
the greater? Cheapnefs of labour, comparative exemption from taxes, and the low
price of the raw material, which were the
motives pleaded for this infufficient protection, are more decidedly in favour of France
than of Ireland.

And

And fingular and extraordinary indeed will it be, if thofe advantages againft which we declared vehemently, when propofed to be granted to our fifter kingdom, fhould be without objection agreed to, when extended to our old enemy and certain rival.

The want of capital in Ireland was the argument principally infifted upon by the fupporters of the Irifh propofitions, as decifive upon the fuperiority of advantage which would refult from them to Great Britain.

Is it poffible to prefume upon this only ground of advantage with refpect to Ireland, when we are fpeaking of a commercial union with France? Such an argument in favour of the prefent treaty, would be too evidently ridiculous to demand a refutation.

Is the French cotton manufactory in a worfe ftate than the Irifh? Is their woollen manufactory no better? Are not their hardware, their hofiery, their glafs, and all their millinery wares, (which owe their value fo much to fafhion) in a ftate a thoufand times more flourifhing, than thofe of

I   Ire-

Ireland ? Yet the manufacturers, of England,
with regard to thefe very points, expreffed
their apprehenfions of the Irifh competition,
and unanimoufly declared, that duties nearly
equivalent to thofe of the prefent French
treaty, were by no means adequate to protect their home manufactures againft this
young and indigent rival. How then is it
poffible, that duties which were totally inadequate in one cafe, fhould be entirely fo
in another, when the circumftances of the
danger are fo much the greater ?

It has been often faid, that the cotton
manufactury is the particular one which is
to gain moft by the opening the French market.

That merchants or fpeculators may for a
time make money by a trade which is a
lofs to the country, is a propofition too
plain to be difputed, and till it can be proved
that the merchant's gain, and the nation's
profit are fynonimous, it will not be neceffary to conteft fo unimportant a fact. But
it may be of fome ufe to take a fhort view
of the ftate of both countries, and to confider

4   for

for one moment, whether that advantage which, if admitted to exist in some articles at present, is of a nature likely to be secure and permanent.

To this end it will be necessary to make a short enquiry into the state of comparative taxation, and price of labour in the two countries.

The principal manufactures of France which are most likely to interfere in the articles permitted to go from England upon custom duties, are settled in the countries of

Normandy,
Picardy,
Britanny,

Flanders,
The Three Bishopricks of Metz,
Toul and *Verden*,
Alsace,
Lorainne,
  and
Hainault.

In

In comparing the taxes of England with
France, it is abſolutely neceſſary that we
ſhould diſtinguiſh between the different provinces of that great empire, becauſe the ſtate
burthens are in no degree like ours, general
and indiſcriminate.—They differ in different
parts of the kingdom, and, therefore, when
we conſider the quantities of taxation to
which the manufacturer is ſubject, it is neceſſary to diſtinguiſh the diſtrict in which he
lives. It may not neceſſarily follow, that the
price of ſubſiſtence is in proportion to the
lowneſs of taxation in each province; but it
happens, however, to be true, in point of fact,
that thoſe diſtricts which we have juſt enumerated, are not only celebrated for the extent
and ſucceſs of their manufactures, but alſo as
being thoſe of all France in which proviſions
are in the greateſt abundance.

Mr. *Neckar* has given an elaborate table of
the different taxes of every ſort paid by the
inhabitants of the different provinces of that
country, and an accurate calculation of the
amount which each individual pays—and from
his ſtatement the following table is taken :

In

TARIFF.	COUNTERVAILING DUTIES.		
	Liv. S.	L s. d.	

In the diftrict which comprehends all Lorrainne and Bar, the taxes amount, per head, to - - -   12 19 = 0 10 9¾

In that of Strafbourg comprehending Alface,   14 1 = 0 11 8½

That of Lifle - - -   20 3 = 0 16 9½

That of Valencienns * - -   20 15 = 0 17 3½

Amiens, which comprehends the country about Calais, Boulogne, and moft of Picardy, - - -   28 10 = 1 3 9

Normandy - - -   29 16 = 1 4 10

Britanny - -   12 10 = 0 10 5

If this rate of taxation be compared with that of England, or even with Ireland, the lownefs of whofe taxes alarmed all the manufacturers of England two years ago, the difference is ftriking and remarkable. By a calculation made by Mr. Walker of Manchefter, and prefented to the Houfe of Peers, it appears that the average amount of taxes paid by the Cotton manufacturers of Lancafhire, amounted to 3 l. per head; if the calculation be extended over the whole of the kingdom, reckoning nine millions of people in Great Britain, the whole amount of our taxes will be equal to 2 l. 7s. or thereabouts, per head; a fum above double the higheft ftate of taxation in any manufacturing province of France, and above

                       four

* Thefe two comprehend all Flanders.

four times the amount of the taxation of the greateſt part of them.

But it is not the lowneſs of taxation alone which the manufacturers of this country have to dread. The wages of labour, and the price of living are equally advantageous to France.

In order to form a juſt compariſon between the rate of the wages of labour in the two countries, we muſt learn the price given for that ſpecies of labour to which the natural faculties of man are equal and applicable, and therefore in the preſent caſe our enquiry ſhould be, what the farmer pays upon an average for a day's labour in both countries. By the beſt information I can obtain, the common wages in the manufacturing parts of France do not exceed 8 or 10 ſous per day, that is, from 4d. to 5d. whereas in England the ſame ſort of labour coſt 1s. 2d. or 1s. 3d. We cannot reaſonably doubt, but there will be nearly the ſame proportionate difference of wages between the manufacturers of the two countries as there is between the day labourers; more eſpecially

especially, when we confider that this lownefs
of the wages of labour is occafioned by lownefs of taxes, and cheapnefs of provifions;
caufes, which equally affect all claffes of men,
as well the manufacturer as the common la-
bourer.—With the joint operation of all thefe
caufes can it be fuppofed that any prefumed
degree of fkill can long countervail fuch decided advantages; capital will find its way to
that fituation where it can be employed to the
beft advantage, and the facility, with which
Britifh artificers are, by the Treaty, enabled
to fettle in France, will, in a fhort time,
give them an eafy poffeffion of our fkill, and
a confequent participation in our capital.

It is to be confidered alfo that the communication between the coafts of England
and France is infinitely eafier, and infinitely
more certain than that between Britain and
Ireland;—from *Calais, Boulogne,* or even
Rouen, Havre, or *L'Orient* to London, the
paffage can rarely exceed a day or two's
navigation, in a fafe and certain channel.
From Ireland the paffage is through a rough
and boifterous fea—dangerous and uncertain
for above half the year, and almoft impracticable

cable to be performed in lefs time than eight
or ten days. Let us paufe upon this circumftance of advantage, and again afk if there
was danger from the Irifh propofitions; and
if 10½ *per cent.* would not have been a protecting duty againft the manufactures of
Ireland, whether it is poffible that the fame
duty can protect our manufactures againft
thofe of France?

The principle alfo upon which countervailing duties are eftablifhed by the treaty,
is narrow, and inadequate. If a countervailing duty have any meaning at all, it is
intended to equalize the burthens under
which the different manufacturers labour, that
they may be upon even terms as to the employment of their refpective fkill, and the
exercife of their mutual induftry.—Will the
countervailing the mere duty impofed upon
the manufacture itfelf, in any fhape produce
the effect which fhould be the vital principle
of this fpecies of protection. It is a melan-
choly truth, with refpect to England, heavily burthened as fhe is, that in the multi-
plicity of her taxes many of them fall equally
fevere upon the manufacturer as if they were
directly

directly imposed upon his manufacture itself.—
The tax upon the house in which the manufacturer lives; the soap and candles, and leather which he uses; the commutation for tea,
which, perhaps, he does not drink; the tax
upon his receipts, his bills, and upon the shop
itself where his goods are sold, must all form
a part of the price of the commodity in
which he deals, and ultimately fall upon the
article equally as if placed immediately upon
it; yet no attempt is made to countervail
such, which are, in fact, virtual *ad valorem*
duties, upon the importation of them.

Were the two countries, *in all respects*, upon
an equal footing, the duties might be sufficient to afford encouragement and protection
to our manufactures; but unequal as they are
in *every* respect to the disadvantage of England, it requires no long look into futurity,
to see the period when her boasted skill,
which at best is but a temporary superiority,
must give way to the influence of advantages
which are certain and permanent.

It is not only that the present treaty is narrow and confined in the principle of its coun-
 K   tervailing

tervailing duties, but that some of the Duties
are totally omitted in the list, such as the duty
upon Leather and upon Malt; while others are
inferted which the minifters themfelves know
it is utterly impoffible to attempt to carry it
into effect, fuch as thofe upon Iron, and Plate
Glafs.

The united teftimony of all the moft re-
fpectable and intelligent manufacturers; when
given before Parliament upon the fubject of
the Irifh propofitions; went, with one voice,
to this opinion, That 10½ per cent. ad valorem,
was totally, and out of all proportion, unequal
to their protection againft the rival manufactures of the fifter kingdom.

If then, as is more than probable, the fame
fyftem of commercial intercourfe between the
two countries fhould be revived again; and if
the manufacturers fhould be found to have
been in a ftate of inaction as to the ac-
complifhment of the prefent Treaty with
France; with what appearance of propriety could they prefent themfelves before
either Houfe of Parliament, to renew their
refiftance to the former meafure?

Would

Would they decline opposing a plan of connection with Ireland, which two years before they had reprefented as pregnant with every fort of danger, and even with certain deftruction to their moft effential interefts?

Or would they have the courage to fay, in the face of fo auguft an affembly, " It is true we contended, that a duty of ten *per cent.* was entirely infufficient to afford us any protection againft the competition of a poor and untaught relation; but we are now equally prepared to argue, That the very fame duty is an ample and fatisfactory fecurity againft the hoftile rivalfhip of a direct enemy, of a Country rich in capital, cheaper in labour, more advanced in fkill, and more abundant in materials."

Would fuch men as Mr. Wedgewood, Mr. Walker, or Mr. Gibbon rifque the fair and honourable refpect which they hold amongft their countrymen, by being guilty of an incongruity fo palpable and difreputable?—They would defpife fuch a proceeding, in words. Let them be careful, then, that they are not equally expofed to the imputation of it, through their

their conduct. If France be only in the same degree of advancement as Ireland, if she possesses labour no cheaper, skill no more improved, or materials in no greater quantities, but all only in the same degree; yet if the communication with England be equally easy and less expensive, how is it that she is not equally a subject of alarm in the formation of a connection, the basis of which, with respect to the manufacturers, is precisely the same.

The manufacturers must explain this in their own vindication—either their opposition to the Irish propositions was *Faction*, or their inertness as to the progress of the present Treaty is *Desertion*; Desertion to the ultimate interests of their country, into which they are seduced by the influence of a little present advantage to themselves.

IRON.

The manufacturers of Iron and Hardware are flattered that their manufacture will find its way into France upon better terms than it formerly did, and an idea is delusively encouraged amongst them, that the high duty upon

the

the import of foreign Iron is to be countervailed upon French goods coming to England. Some high finished, and high priced
articles may, and probably will, for a time,
go from this country to France. They will
do so till British workmen shall teach the
French to avail themselves of the advantages
they possess of the cheapness of their labour,
and the lowness of their taxes. It is in vain,
however, to hope that any of the ordinary forts
of wares can be exported into that country.

The German and *Leige* Hardware, though
perhaps not so highly finished, is infinitely
cheaper than the English. The article of arms
alone, which it has been thought could be purchased at a lower price at Birmingham than in
any part of the world, may be had at Leige
20 *per cent.* cheaper than in England, and other
articles in proportion. The *Flemings* already
excel us in most articles of inferior Hardware;
and can we indulge an expectation that they
will not have at least the same advantage in the
French market which they have in every other?

When Mr. Gibbons, whose authority on
these subjects is certainly of the most respectable nature, was asked by the House of Lords,
whether

whether we had not a confiderable trade in manufactured iron ware to Portugal, Madeira,
and different ports in the Mediterranean? he
anfwered, "That we formerly had—but that
"we had loft it for fome years."

And when afked to affign the reafon of that
lofs, he replied—" The Flemings underfell us.
" They have their labour and their iron cheaper."

Have not the Flemings the fame advantages
in the French as in the Portugueze market?—
Have not the French their labour and their iron
equally cheap as the Flemings?

The duty upon bar iron imported into
France is 15 livres *per* ton, or 12 *s.* 6 *d.*—The
duty upon bar iron imported into England,
amounts to 2 *l.* 16 *s.* 1 *d.* which neither can be
drawn back upon exportation, nor countervailed upon importation.

As both France and England produce iron
of their own, which enters into the manufacture of the country, the power of countervailing the duty upon the raw material, referved
by the treaty, is delufive and impracticable*.

* In point of fact, we know that it is not intended to
be ufed; and, if it could be ufed, it would in France a-
mount nearly to a prohibition upon our goods going there.

When

When a ton of manufactured iron is carried to a custom-house in either country, is it possible to distinguish whether the material is foreign, or British, or French iron—or how much of the one, or how much of the other, enters into the particular quantity of goods manufactured? Yet such distinction must be made, before any drawback can be given, or countervailing duty can be raised. If the goods are of the iron of either the one or the other country, neither drawbacks nor countervailing duties can be made use of, because no duty has, in that case, been paid upon the import of the raw material, and therefore there can be nothing either to drawback or to countervail. If, on the contrary, the goods are manufactured of foreign iron, a drawback ought to be given upon exportation, and the duty ought to be countervailed upon the import.

The absolute impossibility of making those distinctions, places all idea of any countervailing duty totally out of the question. How then, laying for a moment every advantage which France derives from cheap labour and low taxes entirely out of the question) will the account stand as to this article between the two countries.

Mr.

Mr. Gibbons calculates, in his well-informed and ingenious anfwer to Sir Lucius Obrien upon the iron trade, that upon an average it requires a ton and half of iron to produce a ton of manufactured wares. In fome articles it requires more, and in others lefs*.

Let us fuppofe, that a ton thus manufactured is worth 40 _l._ fterling.—Then, Englifh iron going to France will ftand thus :

Duty upon 30 cwt. of iron, manufactured into one ton of wares, at 2 _l._ 16 _s._ 1 _d. per_ ton

Ten _per cent._ upon 40 _l._ duty by the treaty

	£.	s.	d.
	4	4	1½
	4	0	0
	8	4	1½

* The following account of the value of manufactured iron (excluding hardware) is taken from Lord Sheffield's very ingenious and intelligent Obfervations upon the American Trade ; a book which every reader, defirous of knowing the actual ftate of Britifh commerce, ought to confult :

Iron when manufactured is worth per ton;

Bolts	£ 24	Anvils	42
Anchors	30	Tin Plates	42
Nails	35	Steel from 24 to	56
Hoes and Axes	42		

Let

Let us suppose, that the same goods come from France to England.—Then the account will stand as follows :

	£.	s.	d.
French import duty upon 30 cwt. of iron - - -	0	18	9
Ten *per cent.* duty by the treaty	4	0	0
	4	18	9

That is to say, that French wares, manufactured from foreign iron, will come to England 3 *l.* 5 *s.* 4¼ *d.* cheaper than the same goods can go from England to France, and the same sum cheaper than any Englishman can manufacture the same goods from the same iron.— These sums are fully sufficient to prevent English goods going to France, and probably sufficient, when joined to the price of labour, to enable her in time to supply England herself.

But if we should suppose for a moment, that there is little immediate practicability on the part of France to rival us in our own market, let us examine, what is the probability of our supplying hers.

L   It

It is not the Flemings and the Germans only whom we are to meet in the French market,
but the Irish will be enabled to trade there upon terms so infinitely preferable to us, as must
in a very short time give them a decided superiority over us in the French market.

I have already demonstrated the impossibility of either drawing back or countervailing
the import duties upon iron; therefore, Irish
manufactured iron must go to France in the
same way as iron manufactured in Britain now
goes to every part of the world, loaded only
with the import duty upon the material.—The
Irish duty is 9 *s.* 7½ *d. per* ton.

	£.	s.	d.
The duty therefore upon a ton of wares will be	0	14	5¼
Ten *per cent.* duty by the treaty	4	0	0
	4	14	5¼
But English duties on importation into France are	8	4	1½
Therefore the advantage in favour of Ireland is	3	9	8¼

But

But the advantages in favour of Ireland and
of France will be ftill greater than they are
here ftated; as they pay fo much lefs duty,
they can, of courfe, fell their wares cheaper,
in the firft inftance, by all that difference; but
in the fecond, they will evidently have a lefs
per centage duty to pay on the importation of
the fame quantity of manufactured iron.—
The fame ton of wares which in England cofts
40l. and pays a duty of 4l. 4s. 1¼d. paying in
Ireland only 14s. 5¼d. will only pay the 10
per cent. upon 36l. 10s. 3¾d. that is, inftead of paying 4l. will only pay 3l. 13s. 7d.
which makes a farther advantage to Ireland of
6s. 5d. and nearly of the fame fum in favour
of France in the Englifh market.

If to thefe advantages we add that arifing
from cheapnefs of labour, the comparifon will
be ftill more againft this country. Labour in
Ireland is a full third, and in France a full
half, cheaper than in England; and if we
fhould fuppofe, for the fake of calculation,
what is infinitely under the mark, that a ton of
wares value 40l. coft 7l. in England for the

L 2   article

article of labour, the account will then ſtand
thus:

	£.	s.	d.
Duty upon the raw material ſaved in Ireland - - -	3	9	$8\frac{1}{4}$
Saving of duty of 10 *per cent*. upon this ſum, on ſending their wares to France - - -	0	6	5
Saving one-third in the price of labour - - -	2	6	8
£.	6	2	$9\frac{1}{4}$

Such will be the advantage which Ireland
will have over England in manufacturing iron
for the French market. The French and the
Iriſh will be pretty nearly upon a par, as if
labour be ſomewhat cheaper in France than
in Ireland, the duty upon the raw material is
ſomewhat higher in France than in Ireland.—
With theſe advantages, can we ſuppoſe that
France will not rapidly improve in her iron
manufactures; or if ſhe ſhould not, can we
flatter ourſelves that we can have the remoteſt
chance of ſupplying her market; or will not
rather Engliſh artiſts, with Engliſh ſkill and
Engliſh capital, be inclined to emigrate to
Ireland

Ireland for the fake of availing themfelves of fuch a market as that of France.

The idea of drawing back the duty upon the raw material has been often thought of, and as often has been found impracticable. As it cannot be diftinguifhed, whether goods were manufactured from foreign or Britifh iron, the drawing back the duty muft operate, as far as exportation goes, as if no duty were laid upon the import of iron; and it is a known and decided fact, that without fuch duty the valuable iron works in England muft be at an end*.

* An idea has prevailed with fome, that the import of bar iron into this country is much upon the decline, and therefore, that our exports in future will be from iron made in England. The fact is directly the reverfe, the importation of late years has encreafed rather than diminifhed.

Bar Iron imported.

	Tons		Tons		Tons
1764	46,436	1771	48,677	1783	47,914
1765	54,078	1772	51,210	1784	54,457
1766	34,910	1773	48,980	1785	45,600
Average	45,141¼		49,622⅓		49,323⅔

COTTON.

COTTON.

If from the article of iron we proceed to that of cotton, we fhall fee equally little reafon to pronounce a very decided panegyric upon the fkill and intelligence of the negociator of this treaty.

It is a fact pretty well known, that fince the lofs of *Tobago*, which was ceded, perhaps, not with a fingular good policy, by the treaty of peace in 1783 to France, that we have received confiderable fupplies of the raw material from that country, which is fubject to a duty of about 1d. *per lb.* upon export from France.

It is one of thofe fingular derelictions of their own principles which is ·to be found only in minds of fo unftable a ftructure as that of Mr. Eden, that he made no fyftem for fecuring us from the mifchiefs of that peace, which he had been one of the foremoft to reprobate.—His treaty does not contain one fingle ftipulation obligatory upon France, not to encreafe her duties, nor even to bind her againft the entire prohibition of the export of cotton-wool. This power, therefore, is left entirely at her option,

option, and may be exercised whenever she
thinks proper.

Britain imported from France laſt year above
two millions of pounds of cotton; ſhe got
from Portugal nearly the ſame quantity of
Brazil cotton, of a quality, and of a price
ſuperior to any other. Theſe two quantities
amount to nearly one-third of the whole
conſumption of our cotton manufactures*.—
Thus, then, the treaty of commerce which,
by diſguſting Portugal, renders our ſupply
from thence, to ſay no worſe, extremely precarious; and by leaving it in the power of
France to prohibit all ſupply from her quarter,
leaves us at the mercy of our rivals almoſt for
the exiſtence of that manufacture which we
juſtly eſtimate among the moſt valuable of
thoſe our national induſtry is employed in.

France alſo has her cotton at a lower price.
The price of the raw material of this article is
in general from 1d. to 2d. *per lb.* of equal quality, leſs in France than in England. This
originates partly in the ſuperior cheapneſs of

	lbs.
* From France and French Flanders,	2,078,413
From Portugal, - - -	1,629,419

which

her navigation, and partly from the duty which she obliges us to pay for what we export from her.

She has besides many of dying drugs which are employed in this manufacture, of her own growth.

By some unaccountable superiority also of national taste, she excels us in patterns. Many of our present patterns of cottons are designed there, and when they have obtained a greater facility in the manufacture of this article, there is surely a dangerous probability that we shall take from France the stuff instead of the pattern.

The early and successful application of machinery, with the wonderful inventions of Arkwright, (which have, however, been instituted in France with a capital supplied by their treasury, to the amount of 15,000l. to the person who conducts them) joined to the spirit and activity of the manufacturers of Manchester, have hitherto given us a considerable superiority in the cotton trade.—It is clear, however, that the manufacture does not stand upon such grounds as to be above the appre-

4 henfion

henfion of competition. Every advantage
which was dreaded from Ireland, (and a reference to the evidence given before the Houfe
of Lords, on the fubject of the Irifh propofitions, will prove; that the dread entertained
was of the moft alarming nature) is poffeffed
by France; fhe has, or may have, after the
operation of the treaty, every fpecies of machinery equally perfect as at Manchefter.

She has cheap labour, and a multitude of
hands ready to be converted into the beft fort
of workmen in this trade. It was ftated in
evidence upon the Irifh propofitions, that the
beft cotton weavers were bred firft to the
trade of linen weaving, and that a few weeks
were fufficient to qualify them for a proficiency
in it.

The French linen manufacture is extenfive;
Spain and the Spanifh flota are fupplied from
it; and a very little time therefore, if the above
teftimony be founded in fact, and there can
be no reafon to think it is not, will mature her
weavers to the manufacture of cotton.—When
that event fhall happen, we muft lofe at leaft one
market for the purchafe of the raw cotton, and
M   upon

upon what natural or permanent advantage we
can flatter ourfelves with retaining a decifive
fuperiority over a country which will unite
cheaper materials and cheaper labour, with at
leaft equal tafte, it is not eafy to difcover.——
The expectation is too weak for the undiftin-
guifhing fanguinenefs of infancy itfelf.

G L A S S.

In this article it feems quite impoffible to
fuppofe, that we fhould either fupply France,
or continue to fupply ourfelves. Confiderable
duties are paid upon the import of fome articles from which it is made.

And from the mode in which the duty is laid
upon glafs itfelf, it is fcarcely poffible to adjuft a countervailing duty, or fettle a drawback. The duty is charged upon glafs in its
fluid ftate, and no allowance is either made, or
has ever been found practicable to be made,
for the quantity which is ufelefs in the firft
preparation, or what is broken or damaged in
the making. All that quantity not only is
charged with duty in the firft inftance, but is

again

again charged, if it fhould be again thrown into the melting pot. The difference between the real and nominal duty, occafioned by this mode of impofing it, is infinitely various in the different fpecies of glafs ware, and is in fome inftances enormous, but is, at the fame time, impoffible to be afcertained with any fafety to the revenue.

The fame difficulty attends the drawback of duty. In fome inftances, the difference between the drawback and the real duty paid, will amount to 40 or 50 *per cent.* and the difference between the nominal duty and the actual duty paid, is equally great *.

If French glafs coming to England is to pay the duty upon the actual quantity imported, it will be far, indeed, fhort of the duty which

* The proportion between the weight of goods made, and the weight of goods charged by the excife officer, is calculated to be as follows :

Flint glafs   as   100 to 147
Bottle glafs   100 to 112
Broad glafs   100 to 157½

In cut glafs the proportion is infinitely greater; the drawback is in the inverfe proportion; that is to fay, goods which have paid 147, draw back 100.

has

has been paid by the Englifh manufacturer for the fame quantity worked here.

If, on the other hand, it fhould be attempted to form a calculation what the actual duty was which each particular fpecies of wares had paid, it would prove, as all fuch calculations have hitherto proved, a dangerous and impracticable attempt.

Independent of the known fuperiority of the French in many articles of the glafs manufactory, therefore it is not reafonable to expect, that we fhould be enabled to fend any of thofe articles, fuch as crown glafs, in which we are fuppofed to excel all countries, into France. The drawback of duty is lefs than the duty paid on different articles, from 21 to 45 *per cent*; or, in other words, glafs is exported from this country, fubject to a duty from 21 to 45 *per cent*.—Miferable indeed muft be the ftate of the French manufacture, or partial in the extreme muft be the hopes of thofe who can expect to fupply France with glafs ware under fuch circumftances. Ireland labours under none of the above difadvantages; fhe pays no duty upon the raw material, and is improving rapidly in the manufacture of it. Drinking glaffes

may

may be had four or five shilling *per* doz. cheaper in Dublin than in London. If then France is furnished with this commodity from the dominions of his Britannic Majesty, is it to Britain or Ireland that she will direct herself for her supply?

MILLINERY.

This article, though apparently not amongst the most important of those affected by the regulations of the Tariff, will be found to involve as much error in the principle of its adjustment, and as much impolicy as to some of its domestic consequences, as any other included in the operation of the Treaty.

The duty upon this branch of the mutual trade, now for the first time deemed of consequence enough to be comprehended amongst the objects of a general commercial system, is to be in future 12 *per cent. ad valorem* upon importation into either country. Let us examine then, how far this duty is likely to have the effect of a real operative reciprocity.— One principal article of which millinery is composed, is *Muslin*. Muslin bought at the East India Company's sales pays a duty of 18 *l. per cent.* to the Company; of which,

however,

however, 12 _l._ is allowed to be drawn back
on re-exportation.

With refpect to fuch articles of the millinery
as are compofed of the muflin imported by the
French Eaft India Company, this will be the cafe
between the two countries—The French manufacture will have nothing to pay on its importation
here, but fimply the 12 _l. per cent. ad valorem,_
impofed by the treaty. But the fame manufacture of England will have the fix _per cent._
(the difference between the original duty paid
to the Eaft India Company, and the _quantum_
of the drawback) to be added to this reciprocal _ad valorem_ duty; that is, it will pay 18 _l.
per cent._ on its admiffion into the ports of
France. In this view of the fubject, therefore, there is no reciprocity.

With refpect to that part of the French
millinery which is compofed even of muflin
bought in England, they will be found to be
at leaft upon a level with us in our own market. They can purchafe the muflins of the
Eaft India Company, drawing back all the
duty but fix _per cent._ They can return
them in their ftate of finifhed manufacture
                                          here,

here, at the ftipulated duty of 12 *per cent.*;
that is, with the difference only of freight,
which is infinitely overbalanced by the confideration of their cheaper labour, they can
fell their prepared and made up millinery with
every advantage of fuperior fafhion, and every
recommendation of a prevailing partiality in
their favour, precifely for the fame duty
which the Englifhman pays for his unmanu-
factured muflin at the India Houfe.

The almoft entire impoffibility, alfo, which
will exift againft our availing ourfelves of the
permitted drawback on the exportation of the
Company's muflins when fent out in a ftate of
manufacture, will deferve to be confidered.——
An application for the drawback upon the
quantity of this article ufed in the formation of a cap or an apron, will be evidently
difficult to a degree of almoft total impracticability. Upon that fuppofition, the relative
fituation of the two countries as to this
branch of their reciprocal impofts will be this,
That the manufactured muflin fent from England will pay the original 18 *per cent.* to the
Company, and the 12 *per cent. ad valorem* to
the cuftoms of France, making altogether 30
per

per cent. ad valorem, before it can obtain admiffion into their market.—Whereas, as I before ftated, the fame quantity, even of muflin bought from our own Company, can be introduced from France at a duty, only of 18l.
per cent. which leaves a difference of 12l. *per
cent. ad valorem* in their favour; and of 18 l.
per cent. if the muflin be of the importation of
the French Eaft India Company.

Nor does it appear eafy or practicable to
diftinguifh, in many inftances, fo as to adjuft
with precifion, the duty to be paid, on fome
articles at prefent prohibited from France, and
which will in future be imported under the denomination of millinery. India muflins,
French crapes, and tiffanies, are at prefent in
a ftate of prohibition. The former are pofitively admitted by the treaty; and as the latter
may at prefent be imported from Italy, fubject
to a duty, they will with great facility be in
future brought from France, who greatly excel
all nations in thofe manufactures. In a commercial view of this fubject, therefore, it will
appear to be not lefs exceptionable than the
other regulations of the Tariff.—It demands
confideration, however, upon another point of
its inevitable tendency.

Few

Few are the employments which exist in this country for the exercise of female industry,— and few the honest expedients for female subsistence.—Why those should have been wantonly diminished, as by effect of this article they evidently must, and that to a most alarming extent, will not be easily accounted for on any principle of general policy, or with any reconciliation to domestic morals.

Was there not mischief enough done to the male poor of this country, by the operation of the new arrangement, to have satisfied the most systematic Parliament, if any such exist, (or if it be not fairer to suppose ignorance than barbarity) in the negociator of this treaty? —Or, was it a motive of confistency that prevailed with him to the adoption of this pernicious stipulation?—That having uniformly resisted the least appearance of equitable mutuality in the whole course of the negociation with France, he determined to act up to himself, and to reject a reciprocity even in their national gallantry.

Whatever was the cause, the effect is most reprehensible.—If it be true that female virtue

N   be

be a quality which deferves encouragement either as a fource of domeftic happinefs, or public benefit, it muft be equally fo that this part of Mr. Eden's treaty demands the fevereft reprobation, both of the private individual and the politician.

S A D L E R Y.

IT is extremely difficult to afcertain the exact extent of this term.—It is known to comprehend many articles of manufactured leather which by no means appear to be naturally included under it.

Our leather manufacture is certainly at prefent in a more flourifhing ftate than that of the French; but it is equally true, that they are ufing every exertion to arrive at a fpeedy competition with us :—They have all the materials as good, in as great plenty, and as cheap as we have; and there is no fuch myftery in the trade itfelf, as to make it at all difficult of acquifition, more particularly fince the treaty places them on fo advantageous a footing with refpect to it. What appears to be a fifteen *per*

cent.

cent. duty by the treaty, is, in fact, *no duty* at all upon French leather coming to England; but is, at leaft, 25 or 30 *per cent.* upon English fadlery imported there.

The internal duty upon leather in England is equal to about *15 per cent.* upon the value.

It is impoffible to give the fhadow of reafon, why in the lift of countervailing duties this is not to be found. The 15 *per cent.* import duty being then merely equal to the internal duty in this country, puts French and English leather upon the fame footing as if the internal duty had been countervailed, and no duty at the port was to be paid.—

The cafe, however, is directly reverfed upon English leather goods going to France. As the internal duty is paid upon the whole hide, and as confiderable parts of it are loft in the manufacture, the real duty upon the goods is infinitely higher than it appears upon the material.

Three halfpence *per . lb.* upon the whole quantity, may be 2 d. or more upon the ma-

N 2   nufacture.

nufacture. The drawback is only paid upon
the weight actually exported; by which means
a duty of 9 or more *per cent.* remains upon it,
which, added to the port duty in France, of
15 *per cent.* makes the whole duty upon English leather going to France equal to 25 *per
cent.* Whereas I have already said, that by
the operation of our internal duty, French
leather will come here, after paying the 15
per cent. stipulated by the treaty, almost entirely on the same footing with our own,

Of the article of *Porcelain* and *Pottery* I
shall say but little.—The manufactures of
Worcester and *Derby* will certainly be totally
unable to support themselves against the more
beautiful compositions of this article in *Seve*
or *Paris.*

The beauty and elegance of Mr. Wedg-
wood's ware, may for a time give it a confiderable advantage in the French market; but
he has himself declared, upon oath, that no
less a duty than 40 or 50 *per cent.* was sufficient to protect him against the infant manufactures of Ireland :—

That

That it was in the power of any nation, by difficulties at the cuſtom-houſe, by unpacking the goods, and a thouſand ſuch artificial embarraſſments, to convert a low duty into an abſolute prohibition.

That little ſkill was neceſſary in the inferiour workmen;

And that equally little time was neceſſary, in addition to natural advantages and cheapneſs of labour, to transfer the manufacture to another country; of which indeed he gave the remarkable inſtance in Ireland, which, within three years after the trade with America was laid open, had effectually taken from us both the export of leather and of glaſs.

There can be no doubt, therefore, but this manufacture, like others, will only be productive of a temporary advantage to England.

W O O L L E N S.

I come now to that part of the tariff which reſpects the ſtaple of Britiſh manufactures, the trade of her woollens.—It has been a prea prevailing opinion since the publication of Mr. Eden's Treaty, that this is not the part of his system which threatens the most injurious consequences to the manufacturers of Great Britain. General opinions taken up on loose grounds, and disseminated without examination, are apt to have a more deciding influence in this country, than in their nature belongs to them. That this particular species of manufacture is more affected by the stipulations of this treaty, or even equally with some other branches of our trade, I know not, amidst such an accumulation of dangerous innovations, that it would be safe to affirm, That it is not dismissed, however, without some participation in the general defects of this extraordinary arrangement, will not be very difficult to demonstrate.

The *Drap D'Elbeuf*, which is among the finest of the French cloths, sells in that country, as is to be ascertained upon all the most modern authorities, at 19 livres 15 sous, or 16s. 5¼d. according to the present rate of Exchange, per aune.

I need

I need not inform the intelligent reader, but state it to facilitate the enquiries of those who may be less conversant in this sort of information, that the French *aune* is to the English *yard*, in the proportion of nine to seven, that is, it consists of forty-six inches and two sevenths.

By the *Reglemens General, pour la Manufacture du Drap* of August, 1669, and by the *Arret du Conseil*, of the 19th of February, 1671, the most respectable authority, that can be appealed to on this occasion, the breadth of the *Drap D'Elbeuf* is regulated at one aune and $\frac{1}{4}$, or 57 inches $\frac{6}{7}$ in breadth.

By multiplying, therefore, $46\frac{2}{7}$ inches, the length of an aune, by $57\frac{6}{7}$ inches, the breadth of the *Drap D'Elbeuf*, we shall have precisely the number of square inches contained in one aune of this cloth, which upon calculation will be found to be $2677\frac{47}{49}$ square inches.

The price of the best English broad cloth is 18s. per yard, and is 7 quarters or 63 inches in breadth.

The

The length, therefore, as in the former
cafe, multiplied with the breadth, that is,
36 × 63, will give the exact number of fquare
inches contained in one yard of Englifh broad
cloth, which will be found to be 2268 fquare
inches, which will leave a difference of four
hundred and nine fquare inches more cloth
in the aune of *Drap D'Elbeuf*, which fells
for 16s. 5½d. than is in the yard of Englifh broad cloth, which fells for 18s.

By a farther calculation it will appear,
that the fame quantity of fquare inches of
Englifh cloth as are in the French aune, if
fold at Englifh price, would make fuch aune
coft one pound one fhilling and feven pence,
and a fraction. But the French aune of the
Drap D'Elbeuf cofts only fixteen fhillings
and five pence halfpenny; in precifely the
fame quantity of cloth, therefore, there remains a difference in the price to markets,
in favour of France, of four fhillings and
fixpence halfpenny.

To take the calculation another way :—
I have faid that a yard of Englifh broad
cloth cofts 18s. Now it will turn out by a
fimple operation of figures, that the fame

quantity

quantity of French beft cloth, or *Drap
D'Elbeuf*, which is contained in an Englifh
yard, fold at the rate of 16s. 5¼d. per
aune, the French price, would coft precifely
13s. 10½d. per yard. a view of the fubject
which perhaps may make it clearer to the
underftanding of Englifhmen, becaufe more
familiar to the habits of meafurement in
practice amongft them. By this laft calculation then there would remain a difference
per yard between the beft cloths of France
and England, the former indifputably not
inferior in quality to the latter, but directly
the contrary, of 4s. 1½d. in favour of the
Drap D'Elbeuf.

If it fhould be urged in reply to the above
facts, which certainly ftand upon evidence,
that it will be very difficult, if at all practicable to fhake, that though the difference
of price of the fame quantity of the fame
fort of cloth, between the two countries, be
certainly material, yet it is not fo much as
will not be fufficiently covered by the duty
of 12l. per cent. united with the expence
of freight, &c. which may be fairly eftimated
at 3l. more, and which will make the whole
amount of the charges upon importation here

O   of

of French woollens 15l. per cent. *ad valorem.* This it may, and indeed has been said will be such an incumbrance upon the admiffion of cloth, as to amount pretty nearly to a mutual prohibition. How far that is likely to be the cafe with refpect to the Britifh market, it will be my next bufinefs to enquire.

Suppofe it to be admitted upon the average, and it cannot be far from the mark, but at all events is equally fair between the two countries, that two yards and a half of Britifh broad cloth are taken up in making one coat.

	£.	s.	d.
We have feen, that the fame quantity of the *Drap D'Elbeuf* which is contained in an Englifh yard, cofts	0	13	$10\frac{1}{2}$
A coat of this therefore, made on the average mentioned above, will coft precifely	1	13	$8\frac{1}{4}$
A coat made of the fame quantity of Britifh cloth, at the market price, to wit, 18s. per yard, will coft	2	5	0

Which

Which will leave a difference of eleven shillings and three pence three farthings on each coat.

Now 15 *l. per cent. ad valorem*, upon 1 *l.* 18 *s.* 8¾ *d.* the price of the coat made of the *Drap d'Elbeuf*, will amount to 5 *s.* and a fraction. This added to the price, will make the whole cost upon importation into England, precisely 1 *l.* 18 *s.* 8¾ *d.* that is 6 *s.* 3¼ *d.* less than a coat made of our own broad cloth in the metropolis of England.

It is proper to observe here, that there is great reason to believe, after the operation of this treaty, cloaths will be imported into this country, in great quantities, ready made; in which case will be to be added, to the other advantages in favour of France, the decided superiority they possess over us, in the essential article of cheaper labour. It is well known as a fact, that a coat is made in Paris for four livres 10 sous, or 3 *s.* 9 *d.* English, which in London will cost at least 10 *s.* 6 *d.*

In the whole of the above argument I have totally left out of the question all consideration

of fuperior quality on the part of the French
fuperfines; a fact, however, which is fufficiently attefted, and will not (particularly in their
Scarlets and their Blacks, in which we do not
come within the remoteft chance of competition) be attempted to be controverted by any
perfon at all converfant in thefe concerns.

I fhall next inquire, whether the manufactures of our own wool are likely to be fent in
large quantities to France; and for that purpofe it will be neceffary to examine, whether
the difference in the price of the raw material
in the two countries, is fo much in favour of
England, as as to enable her to fend her manufactures of coarfe wool in competition to the
French market, where labour is fo much cheaper, and under an expence of 15 *l. per cent.*

Lord Sheffield, in his Obfervations on Trade
with the American States, fuppofes common
wool 20 *per cent.* cheaper in England than in
France. This gives us an advantage of 5 *l.*
per cent. at the French market; but this 5 *l.*
per cent. is not only no very great encouragement, but it is certain that, from recent advantages acquired by France, this fuperiority is not

now very confidently to be relied upon. France has gained upon us, in this fpecies of woollen, in the Levant market, for a long time. It is equally well afcertained, that our trade to the fouth of Europe has declined to a very large degree.— We confoled ourfelves with the hope, however, that it would maintain itfelf in the north of Europe*; but it has decreafed in that quarter (taking an average of four years following the year 1763, and of the four years ending 1784) from 1,331,928 *l.* to 573,029 *l.* A part of this great deficiency muft be fupplied from fome other quarter; for all the countries which we previoufly furnifhed with this article certainly cannot fupply themfelves. The woollen manufactures of Spain are confiderably improved†; but ftill fhe does not produce fufficient, even for her own dominions. We therefore know of no country that can fupply what

---

* Namely, in Holland, Germany, Ruffia, Denmark, Sweden, and the Eaft country.

† Efpecially in bays, low cloths, and ferges, which are cheap, though of an inferior kind. Some of her ferges indeed are at leaft as good as ours. The fhalloons made at Guadaxaro, ten leagues from Madrid, are very good, though not well preffed or finifhed.

we

we have loft, unlefs it fhould be France.—In the long bays, and other branches of the Bocking manufacture, fhe decidedly excels us. As good camblets as any in the world, are now made at Lifle. She can alfo underfell us in a manufacture between camblet and bartagon, worn by the clergy. She is enabled to carry on a large manufacture of fine ferges in Normandy and Brittany ; and alfo of fagathies at Amiens, Abbeville, and other places. She furpaffes us at prefent in the dreffing of beavers, worn for great coats ; and they now at leaft equal us in mixed colours, in which we ufed to excel.

I fhall now proceed to fay a few words in the way of calculation upon the Cloths of inferior quality, and to avoid too particular a detail (the prolixity of which may, I fear, have, by this time, fufficiently fatigued the Reader; but let it be always remembered, however, that, in fubjects of this kind, it is upon minute points that great interefts folely hinge) will content myfelf with confidering only *one* fort, in which both countries carry on a very extenfive manufacture ; I mean the *Silefias.*

The

The French *Silesia,* which is, beyond all comparison, a lighter and pleasanter, and even finer Cloth than ours of the same denomination, costs 6 liv. 10 sous, or 5s. and 5*d. per aune,* in Paris, and is ¼ of an aune in breadth ; the English *Silesia* costs 6s. *per yard* in London, and is ¼ of a *yard* in breadth.

Pursuing the same kind of calculation that was adopted in the former instance, it will appear that there is contained in one aune of French Silesia, which is sold for 5s. and 5d. 634 $\frac{18}{45}$ more square inches than is contained in the English yard, which is sold for 6s.

It will appear farther, that the same number of square inches of English Cloth which is contained in the French aune, if sold at the English price, would cost precisely 9s. 10¼d. and that the same quantity of square inches of French Silesia which is contained in one English yard, would, at the French price, cost 3s. 3¼d. that is to say, the French Silesia is exactly 3s. 2¼d. cheaper per English yard than English Silesia.

The quality of the French is unquestionably superior;—the price is little more than -

half,

half, and yet an opinion is delusively diffused, and unwarily credited, That no injury of any kind is to be sustained to any department of our Woollen manufactures by the operation of Mr. Eden's Treaty.

I cannot, however, admit the supposition that there is so fixed a system of irrational credulity in my fellow-subjects, or so criminal a negligence in the Woollen manufacturers, both as to their country's interest and their own, as to think it possible after the above representation, unless the facts, on which it stands, can be subverted, that the one will continue to indulge, or that the other will persevere in a passive acquiescence, in so pernicious a misconception *.

THE TRADE WITH SPAIN.

The discussion of this part of the Tariff naturally leads us into an examination of what will be the probable operation of the Treaty upon our Commerce with Spain, the country

* The reader will find the general argument on Woollens very intelligently stated, in a plain, but well-informed production, entitled *The Woollen Draper's Letter*, published by Debrett.

from

from whence, we need not inform the Reader
who has followed us thus far in our Remarks,
that species of Wool is imported, of which
the whole of our superfine Cloths are entirely fabricated.

The Trade between this country and Spain,
unhappily for us, has been, for some years,
most alarmingly on the decline. — The following is an estimate of its exports and imports in the years

1775,	1776,	1783	1784:
1,205,215 2 9	1,191,477 19 3	589,887 13 18	802,246 3 0
564,386 6 0	561,071 11 9	419,462 4 1	637,337 9 11
£. 640,928 16 9	630,406 7 6	170,425 9 7	164,908 13 1

To which is to be added the produce of the
Fish trade from Newfoundland, which being in the number of what are called the
enumerated articles, is exported from that
Island without coming into the ports of
Great Britain, and therefore is not included
in the estimates of our Customs, and which
in some years has amounted to 337,028
quintals. The price of this in the ports of
Spain, inclusive only of their own duty upon
importation, is 18 s. per quintal, which will

P   which

leave a fum of 303,327l. to be added with the reduction, as we have faid, of their internal duty, to the amount of our exports.

This diminution is to be accounted for from the combined influence of the follow-ing caufes :—

1ft. From the encreafed fafhion of French and Portugal wines, which has leffened the im portation of thofe of Spain into this country, in a comparifon between the year 1700 and 1785, in the proportion of more than five to one.

2d. From the operation of the regulation of 1782, which equalized the duty upon all foreign brandies from wherefoever imported. —Previous to this period, the brandies of Spain came into this country at a confiderably lower duty than thofe of France ; but being inferior in quality, as well as being attended with a much heavier expence of freightage, they could not ftand a competition, when placed on a footing of equalized duty, and are now in a ftate of virtual prohibition.*

3d.

Per Ton.

£.   s.   d.

* Before the year 1782 the cuftom-houfe duty
   upon French brandy was   -   -   -   8   5   6
That upon Spanifh   -   -   -   4   8   6

By

3d. From the participation and preference of France in their market for woollens, And 4thly, From the inftitution of feveral manu-factures in that article, in their own country.

This decreafe is the more to be lamented, as our trade with Spain, both as to the imports and exports, was conducted on a footing the moft advantageous which can poffibly fubfift between two diftinct empires.—We took nothing from them but raw materials or articles of native produce; fuch as their wines or brandies, upon which no labour could be employed.—They took from us various defcriptions of our made-up articles, and even large quantities of their own raw materials returned to them in a ftate of complete and finifhed manufacture. — We had their wool, cochineal, indigo, and barilla, which we fent back again to the country of their original produce in bales of cloth of different denominations. By a double operation of advantage, therefore, we made them pay the price of our labour, and had their market for the fale of a Britifh manufacture, the conftituent materials

By an act paffed in 1782, the cuftom duty upon *all* brandy is 8l. 8s. per ton, which with the 5 *per cents*. is now 9l. 4s. 6d.

                   of

of which were produced in their own country.
The balance of this trade, therefore, was always
to the advantage of England; and the furplus,
amounting generally to near a million annually, was conftantly remitted to us in actual
fpecie.—To fay nothing that the materials
which are imported from them were fuch as
we could not poffibly do without—fome of
which we could get no where elfe, and others
from no other country except Portugal, in
fimilar perfection or with equal advantage;
and all of which were fo indifpenfibly effential
to us, that without them the whole of our ftaple manufacture, our national trade of woollens, muft have ftagnated or ceafed.

It is difficult to afcertain, what may be the
future revolutions in the tafte or character of
a country.—It is not, therefore, out of the
number of poffible events, that Spain might
herfelf become a great manufacturing kingdom, and might employ her own fubjects in
the working her own materials. But till fuch
a difpofition had began to prevail with them—
till intereft had infpired induftry, and till induftry had been matured by experience, it is
clear to demonftration, that Spain was, of all the
countries in Europe, that with whom it was

                                        moft

moſt particularly the advantage of England,
and moſt preſſingly the duty of her Rulers to
have cultivated an intercourſe, and to have
cemented a friendſhip.

A very different policy, however, has evidently influenced the negociator of the preſent
Treaty.—A ſinking trade demands to be protected and ſuſtained. It is much to be feared,
and infinite will be the cauſe of regret, if the
event ſhould turn out ſo to be, that the effect
of this new ſyſtem can terminate only in giving the laſt blow of deciſive ruin, to a branch
of commerce already weak and languiſhing,
yet ſtill important and advantageous.

The brandies of Spain are already in a ſtate,
as has been before ſaid, of virtual prohibition
from this country.—Their wines, by the operation of the Treaty, will be pretty nearly
in a ſimilar ſituation.—Even the circumſtance
of a more prevailing degree of faſhion in the
French wines, has been ſufficient to diminiſh
the conſumption of thoſe of Spain, in the proportion of at leaſt five to one, in the courſe of
little more than eighty years, as may be ſeen
by the computation taken from the Inſpector-
General's books at the Cuſtom-houſe.

Spaniſh

Spanish Wines imported into England from
Christmas 1699, to Christmas 1701.

		Tons.	Hog.	Gall.
1699	—	11,701	3	60
1700	—	13,649	—	7
1701	—	11,184	2	17

Ditto imported into England from Christmas
1783, to Christmas 1785.

		Tons.	Hog.	Gall.
1783	—	2,149	1	23
1784	—	2,553	3	41
1785	—	2,534	1	34

At each of these periods, and during the
whole of the interval which took place between
them, the import duty upon Spanish wines was
about 18 shillings *per ton* more than that upon
the wines of Portugal; that is to say, some-
what *less than half* of that which existed upon
the wines of France. If then, by the mere advantage of preferable quality, or more congenial taste and flavour, the wines of France
could occasion so material a diminution in the
consumption of those of Spain as has been
proved above, is it auguring either rashly or

factiously

factioufly to fuppofe, that when the duty upon the French wines fhall become only one-half of what it was formerly, and the duty upon the wines of Spain fhall remain the fame, it will produce an almoft entire abolition of the ufe of them ?—A fmaller advantage, than this, when extended to French brandies by the act of the equalization of duties in the year 1782, totally deftroyed the confumption of Spanifh brandies in this country. On what ground, then, either of general argument or analogy, can we poffibly prefume that a fimilar effect will not follow from a regulation, which, though not exactly of the fame kind, is certainly more injurious to the importation of their wines.

If that event fhould take place, and the wines of Spain fhould ceafe to be ufed in England, this then would be precifely the fituation of the commerce between the two countries. Every article and iota of it, both as to importation and exportation, will be totally and exclufively in favour of Great Britain. We fhall receive nothing from them but what we cannot poffibly do without, and they will continue to take from us without the moft remote

pretenfions

pretenfions to a reciprocity, or the fhadow of
an inducement, what they can very well continue to import from other countries. Is it to
be reconciled to any principle of common
fenfe, or any experience of the practice of
States, to fuppofe that things fhould remain
long in fuch a fituation. They have a fevere
power of retaliation in their own hands, and
will certainly have every motive for the exercife of it.

Indeed a review of the circumftances under
which we have enjoyed the free importation
of the wool of Spain down to this time, will
abundantly prove that fhe has never granted
us that indulgence without a fufficient and
adequate inducement, and that, therefore, fhe
is not likely to perfevere in fo doing when that
inducement no longer exifts. The firft commercial treaty of any extent that we had with
that kingdom was executed in the year 1667,
and is generally known by the name of Lord
Sandwich's treaty, though principally negociated
under the direction of Sir *W. Godolphin*, Secretary
to the embaffy. Sir W. was fo confcious of its
importance to this country, that in his letter
to the minifter, containing the intimation of

its ratification, he thus expreſſes himſelf with
an honeſt triumph : " The treaty of com-
" merce, I dare promiſe your Lordſhip, com-
" prehends not only all the privileges and ad-
" vantages which this crown hath ever granted
" to any other ſtate or people, but likewiſe
" ſome conveniencies which it hath never yet
" permitted to any other."—Alluding point-
edly to the unimpeded exportation of the Spaniſh wool.—The ſervice performed by Sir
William, in obtaining this advantage, was
deemed of conſequence enough to incline the
miniſtry three years afterwards, in 1670, to ap-
point him ambaſſador plenipotentiary to the
court of Madrid, with a view of renewing this
ſame treaty, for the value of it began to be
very ſenſibly perceived—This was accordingly
done.—Now it is to be obſerved, in the firſt
place, upon this event, that at that time the
manufacture of French woollens was entirely
in its infancy, and therefore Spain had no
market for that part of her produce in that
country. Indeed no other vent exiſted for it
in Europe at that period but England; and
though the importation of it, therefore, was
an evident advantage to us, it was hardly leſs
ſo to her.—It is to be attended to alſo as a co-

Q   operating

operating motive for this indulgence, that
our imports of her wine and brandy, were at
that period immenfe. So far, therefore, her
kindnefs was not without an adequate inducement.—The next revival of this treaty took
place in the year 1713, the æra of the famous
treaty of Utrecht, for even the defpifed and
perfecuted negociators of that reprobated en-
gagement were not either weak or wicked
enough to confign a participation of our trade
to France, without taking care that a fecurity
for the importation of the material upon which
our woollen manufacture totally depended,
was firft provided. The circumftances, however, between England and Spain had not
much changed, and, therefore, the fame motives were applicable to this extenfion of her
indulgence with refpect to the wool, that
were mentioned in the former inftance.

The treaty of 1667 was again renewed in
1750 *. By this time, however, our importion
of Spanifh wines and brandy had very confiderably diminifhed; indeed between the years

* The three articles of the treaty of Utrecht, generally
called explanatory, were revoked by Mr. Keen's treaty,
and that of 1667, renewed in *toto.*

1740

1740 and 1748 they had been much lefs than
at prefent, and another market for her wool
had began to prefent itfelf in France. She
became confcious, therefore, of the favour fhe
had fhewn us, and determined to make an adequate advantage of it.—By the treaty of *Aix la*
Chapelle, concluded the year before, we were in
poffeffion of the Afiento contract for Negroes,
a miferable traffick, of which we made a ufe perfectly congenial to the principle of the trade itfelf. It was highly important to Spain to get
this contract out of our poffeffion, and fhe
fent over a propofition, in which fhe agreed to
allow us one hundred thoufand pounds in
money, and as a farther inducement, to *renew*
the *commercial treaty* of 1667, as a price for
relinquifhing the injurious intercourfe with her
colonies.—The terms were accepted, and the
treaty was accordingly ratified at Madrid,
under the direction of Mr. *Keene*.—This is the
laft inftance of any fpecific or formal renovation of the treaty in queftion, although it has
been twice revived fince by a fweeping claufe
in each of the treaties of peace that have taken
place fubfequently.

It is as clear therefore as historical evidence can make it, that Spain never granted the free importation of her wool into this country, but under the influence of some equivalent advantage ; either direct or collateral. Is she likely to be equally indulgent to us in a state of provocation and injury, as in a situation of reciprocal benefit and conciliation ? Is there any one so weak in his devotion to the politics of Mr. Eden, as to admit a supposition so revolting to the understanding, and so repugnant to the known conduct of States ?

If then, actuated by a natural and justifiable resentment towards this country, inclined by the tie of family amity towards France, and urged by the reflection that she has no longer an advantage in a commercial intercourse with Great Britain, Spain should impose a prohibition, or a prohibitory duty on the importation of her wool into England, what would be the consequence ?

It would require all the industry of Mr. Eden to make out the detail of so comprehensive a mischief, and much more than his
                                        judg

judgment or talents to produce a compenfation for it. It almoft exceeds belief, and
tranfcends perhaps all recorded precedent of
inattention or incapacity, that a man fhould
make an alliance with a natural enemy, to
the difadvantage of a natural friend ; that
that friend fhould be in the poffeffion of
an article without which the perfon making
fuch alliance could not live nor fubfift, and
yet that he fhould never folicit the poffeffion
of it before the intention of his new en-
gagement was openly announced, nor make
any provifion to deprecate a refentment, the
effects of which would be fatal to his neareft
interefts, till he had given every provocation
of the moft pointed neglect, and fupplied
every motive of the moft defencible recri-
mination, for the fulleft and moft unqualified
exertion of it.

Such has been the conduct of Mr. Eden
with refpect to England, France, and Spain.
—If the confequence of his management
be any thing lefs than the entire deftruction of the manufacture of our fineft and moft
valuable woollens, the Country muft owe to accident or felicity what it has failed of fe-

curing

TARIFF.

curing, by the intervention of his care and
fagacity.*

CAMBRICK.

The duties by the treaty impofed upon
French cambricks are another proof of the inattention of the Negociator to what has been
the policy of this country in times paft. Formerly, while they were allowed to be imported
under a confiderable duty, the manufacture was
utterly unknown in Britain. Since the prohi-

* That the reader may judge of the nature of our imports from Spain, and how much they confift in raw materials, I fhall fubjoin one year's imports from thence.

Spanifh Wool	1,861,231	⎫
Indigo	396,400	⎪ lbs.
Cochineal	147,845	⎬
Cortex Peru	33,969	⎭
Fruit	11,618,500	No.
Wine	2,534	Tons.
Raifins	60,423	Cwt.

Our exports confift entirely of woollen goods; pilch-
ards, falmon, tin, butter, beef and pork from Ireland.
Of Woollens alone England, in the year 1768, exported to Spain to the value of 952,438l. and in the
year 1775 to that of 862,000l.

bitory

bitory act 18 Geo. II. c. 36. it has been by
flow degrees increasing in Scotland and in Ireland ; and lately the progress it has made has
been confiderable. There were stamped for
fale, in Scotland, in the year 1783, 56,304
yards; in 1784, 83,438; in 1785, 106,755.
Under the prefent duty, this rising manufacture
must be utterly ruined ; whereas it might have
been protected, and a confiderable revenue fecured, by laying higher import duties upon
French cambricks, at the fame time that they
need not have been fo high, as either to prevent the importation, or encourage fmuggling.

As the manufacture of the inferior forts of
cambrick is that which is most likely to fucceed in Scotland, and as the chief view of
France is to fecure the market of England for
her fine cambrics, the object of both countries
would have been fecured, by laying the duty in
fuch a manner as to exclude the coarfer, at the
fame time that it admitted the importation of
the finer.

It has been fuggested that a duty of 8 s. per
demi-piece would effectually anfwer this purpofe, have protected the Scotch and the Irish
manufactures,

manufactures, and have afforded a considerable revenue to the public.

Though the linen manufacture of France is
in so flourishing a state as completely to supply
both Spain and Portugal with the immense
quantities of coarse linens they consume, yet it
is not very probable, under the present duties,
that either the Irish or the British linen manufacture have any thing to apprehend from the
importation of French linen: though it may
be probable that Britain, in future, will take
from France considerable quantities of some
sorts of linen which she now imports from the
north of Europe; a circumstance which considerably increases one of the worst tendencies of
the present treaty, the throwing all the commerce of England into one channel, and the
disobliging every nation with whom we now
carry on trade, in order to encourage the manufactures of France.

There is at present in France a demand
for some sorts of Irish linen, and considerable
quantities are now smuggled there. It might
have been thought a fair advantage for our sis-
ter kingdom, while we ruined her rising manufacture of cambrics, that some sort of advantage

tage fhould have been ftipulated in her favour for thofe fpecies of her linens which are in requeft in France. All forts of Linens howevre are virtually prohibited going from Ireland to France by the treaty; for it is well known, that the Irifh duties upon Dutch linens are in their nature prohibitory; and therefore, the duties upon Irifh Linens going to France will be alfo prohibitory. And thus, by the terms of the treaty, while the Irifh are taught to expect a benefit, the fubftance of the article is a mockery to them, and an exclufion to their ftaple manufacture.

———

Having gone through the principal articles of the tariff, it is neceffary to inform the reader of one objection which pervades the whole; which is, that although the duties impofed upon articles carried from the one country to another, appear upon the face of them to be reciprocal in amount; and although French goods coming to Britain, and paying the import duty, are from that moment free from any farther charge whatfoever—yet the cafe is directly the reverfe with Britifh goods going to France; which in many inftances will have to pay additional duties to thofe impofed by the

R   tariff,

tariff, and higher ones than fimilar goods of the manufacture of France.

When any commodity is imported into France, and pays a fpecific duty of *entré*, at whatever part of the kingdom it may be imported, this is called a *Droit uniforme*, the effect of which is to protect the goods from all internal duties, or, as they are called in France, *Droits du circulation*, till they arrive at the place of their original deftination : but once arrived there, if they are again to be carried from one part of the kingdom to another, they become fubject to all the different local duties which prevail in different parts of that great kingdom, and thefe duties are in almoft every inftance higher upon foreign, than upon French manufactures. Thus, if a bale of Englifh woollens be fent from London to Lyons, the twelve per cent. paid at importation will protect it from all duties till it arrives at the place to which it is addreffed. But if the merchant at Lyons has occafion to tranfport the fame bale of goods to Aix or to Marfeilles, it will become fubject to frefh duties, confiderably higher than a French bale of the fame goods would pay.

These

These are shackles imposed upon the commerce of England to France, in which there is no reciprocity. If the French merchant misses his market in one place, he may move his goods to another, and so on through every town in Britain, without being subject to any duty or imposition whatsoever.

REVENUE.

I have now gone through the principal articles in the Tariff; and from the review of it, the reader will already have anticipated me in concluding, That there is scarcely a manufacture which is not endangered; an important foreign trade which is not placed in the hazard of ruin, nor many branches of the Revenue which can escape its destructive influence. It is difficult to calculate all the losses to the public purse from so complicated and extensive an innovation; all which, however, can be positively ascertained are alone such as I shall state here, and they will appear as follows:

R 2

Loss

REVENUE.

	£.	s.	d.
Lofs of 50 *l. per* ton on French wine - - -	20,098	6	8
Lofs ⅟₇ prefent duty on Portugal wine - - -	161,404	18	2
Lofs of 2*s.* 6*d. per* gallon on Brandy imported - -	90,951	8	6
Lofs of 5*s. per* gallon on Rum	35,826	12	1
Lofs of 2*d. per* gallon on malt fpirits - - -	26,128	3	2
	£. 334,400	8	7

It has, indeed, been faid, that the duties eftablifhed by the Tariff will be fufficiently productive to compenfate for this enormous lofs ; but I have already proved that they cannot be productive in the articles in which the lofs arifes without involving the ruin of the Portugal trade, and the deftruction of the Weft India planter, and Home Diftillers, and giving rife to confequences, both to trade and revenue, far more extenfive than it is poffible to form an eftimate of, at this time. If the duties upon the other articles are to be productive, it can only refult from the immenfe importation of

French

French Woollens, Cottons, Hardware, Sadlery, or other manufactured articles which directly and immediately interfere with fimilar
articles of our own, and by fo doing, affect
every excifeable commodity in the kingdom, to
an extent far beyond what any port duty can
make good.

SMUGGLING.

It has alfo been fuggefted that the duties
eftablifhed by the Treaty will effectually put
an end to the fmuggling of foreign articles,
and by that means produce a compenfation for
all the apparent defalcation to the Revenue.—
How far that expectation is likely to be real-
ized by the event, it fhall be my next fubject
to enquire.

The fact is, indeed, that it is not only from
thofe goods, which may be lawfully imported
under the prefent Treaty, that the trade of
England has reafon to be alarmed; the cafe
and fafety which it extends to fmuggling, is
fufficient to render, almoft nugatory, every
fecurity which the fair trader poffeffes, from
prohibitions,

prohibitions, and every advantage which the revenue derives from high duties.

The prohibited articles of silks, gold and
silver stuffs, lace of every sort, are so small
in bulk and so valuable in themselves, that if
there was nothing more than an increased
intercourse between the two countries, the
preventing their being smuggled in great
quantities would be totally impracticable.—
The only risk of seizure is on the landing ; because, as similar fabrics are produced by our
own manufacturers, it is impossible for the
officers of the revenue to distinguish the one
from the other ; and if a constant and considerable trade is carried on between the two
countries, those articles, in such estimation with
the rich and the fashionable, will easily find
their way amongst us, to the ruin of our own
manufactures, of the same species.

There are, however, in the Treaty, some
regulations which totally annihilate most of our
useful Laws against smuggling, and which
more particularly militate against that act
which Mr. Eden himself had a principal
share

ſhare in propoſing, and in procuring to be paſſed.

By the nineteenth Article of the preſent Treaty it is ſtipulated, That.

The ſhips of either party being laden, ſailing along the coaſts of the other, and being forced by ſtorm into the havens or ports, or MAKING LAND THERE IN ANY OTHER MANNER WHATEVER, ſhall not be, obliged to unlade their goods, or any part thereof, or to pay any duty, unleſs they, of their own accord, unlade their goods there, and ſell ſome part thereof.

By the tenth Article they are not to be ſubject to any forfeiture for any defect or omiſſion in the entries of their goods ;— and by the twenty-fifth,

The ſhips belonging to the ſubjects and inhabitants of the reſpective kingdoms coming to any of the coaſts of either of them, but without being willing to enter into port, or being entered, yet not willing to land their cargoes or break bulk, ſhall not be obliged to give an account of their lading, unleſs they are ſuſpected, upon ſure evidence, of carrying prohibited goods, called contraband, to the enemies of either of the two high contracting parties.

How can any of theſe articles be carried into effect without a repeal of our preſent laws / which have been found abſolutely neceſſary for the protection of the revenue ?

By

By the 24th Geo. III. 47. every veſſel hovering, (that is not proceeding directly upon her voyage) and having on board any brandy in caſks under 60 gallons, or any other goods whatſoever ſubject to. forfeiture, may be ſeized if found within four leagues of the coaſt.

And every veſſel of a particular conſtruction, which are ſuppoſed favourable to ſmuggling, are prohibited to be uſed by any Britiſh ſubject, unleſs by licence.

By other laws, every veſſel is obliged to make an entry of her cargo, if it be of a nature which is enterable ; and it has been found neceſſary to enact, that they ſhould be ſubject to forfeiture, in caſe ſuch entry ſhould be found to be defective or erroneous.

It is ſelf-evident that, at leaſt ſo far as regards French ſhips, all theſe laws muſt be repealed.

In future they may make land in any manner they pleaſe.

They are not obliged to enter their cargoes.

They

They may come upon the coasts, and either come into port or not, as they chuse.

They are not obliged to give an account of their lading, except in the single case of their being *suspected upon sure evidence* of carrying prohibited goods to the enemy.

And they may use vessels of any construction, however adapted to smuggling, and however prohibited to be used by British subjects. The description in the twenty-fifth article, viz. of ships coming upon the coasts without being willing to enter into port, is the precise and accurate definition of hovering, and is by the treaty permitted.

The alarming heighth to which smuggling has arrived, has made it necessary to enact, that the merely being within certain limits, with certain goods on board, shall be of itself a cause of forfeiture; but in future, as the cargoes are not permitted to be examined, a French smuggler, lying at the back of Dover harbour, laden with brandy in small casks, is not liable to be seized, unless taken in the very act of landing her cargo.

S

Can

. .Can we entertain a doubt, that under such circumstances, the smuggling of not only such articles as are prohibited, but of such articles as are admissible under high duties, must increase to an enormous amount ?—Our silk manufacture, which has been often injured by the clandestine importation of French silks, must be totally ruined; and the stipulated diminution of the duties upon brandy, can have but little effect in preventing its being smuggled.

.The duty of 7 s. *per* gallon is about 500 *per cent.* upon the prime cost, which is about 1 s. 4 d. in France; and, under all the restrictions of hovering acts, and restraints of custom-house laws, we have the authority of the Committee on Smuggling for saying, that it could be afforded upon the coasts of Britain for 3 s. *per* gallon. When such a price left profit sufficient to the smugglers, under all the risks which he was formerly exposed to, he will undoubtedly be able to sell it still cheaper, when those impediments are removed; and whether the duty be 7 s. or 9 s. 6 d. will make little difference, as there is still a sufficient profit to encourage him in the practice, and to secure him against risks, which are now hardly to be considered as any longer dangerous.

In

SMUGGLING.

In future, indeed, all the contraband trade will be carried on in French veffels; for it is they only who will be free from all the reftraints of the various laws we have mentioned.

There is another fpecies of fmuggling which has of late been much practifed, and which alfo in future may be carried on with confiderable advantage—I mean that of drawback and certificate goods.

If a French veffel fails from the Thames laden with goods, upon which fhe fecures the drawback, fhe may fail round the ifland, come upon the coaft as fhe pleafes, is not liable even to be examined, and may fettle her plans of operation with the fmugglers on fhore, till fhe finds the convenient opportunity of landing her cargo; and is not feizable, except in the very act of fmuggling.

Under thefe advantages, joined to the more extenfive communication between the two countries, it is utterly impoffible to fuppofe, that the revenue can be at all productive in any article under high duties; or that any of thofe manufactures which we have found it neceffary to protect, either by prohibitions or by high duties, can continue even to exift.

Such is the foundation of the hope which has been so induftrioufly encouraged, and fo precipitately entertained, that all the future injuries to the revenue, and many more befides thofe immediately refulting from this treaty, were to be made good by the entire extermination of fmugglers from the borders of the empire.

DROIT D'AUBAINE.

It is not meant to be here contended, that this is one of thofe Articles of the Treaty which tends equally with feveral others of it, to the radical fubverfion of the national interefts. In as much, however, as the nature of fuch a regulation will permit the poffible exiftence of injury, fo far precifely it is the tendency of the prefent modification of it to encourage every difadvantage.

I need not inform, but may be indulged in reminding the intelligent reader, that the *Droit D'Aubaine* is a privilege exifting in France, by which the King of that country claims a right to all the perfonal property of an *alien* who fhall die in his dominions. It will be much lefs neceffary for me to obferve to any

perfon

perfon at all converfant in the laws or ufages of this country, that no privilege at all corref-ponding to the above, prevails in England.

If this right were rigidly carried into ef-fect in France, it would be rather to be confi-dered as an advantage than an injury to Great Britain, as in that cafe it would have the falu-tary operation of preventing emigration. If it were totally abrogated, as is recommended by Mr. *Neckar*, this confolation (which though evidently inadequate, is the beft which the cir-cumftances admit) would refult from that ar-rangement of it. That an inhabitant of Eng-land who had taken up his refidence in France, might enjoy the fatisfaction at laft, and his country the benefit, of reftoring the whole of his property by his will to his heir, or other ob-ject of his preference in his native land.

The worft poffible fituation in which this privilege can be placed, is that of doubt or ambiguity, and in that Mr. Eden has com-pletely left it ;—fo left it, that every injury refulting from the firft hypothefis I have laid down, remains in its full extent, while the be-nefit fecured by the latter, is at beft precarious

and

and doubtful. The temptation to emigration remains in full force, but the reftoration of property is expofed to the uncertain juftice of a French Judge, deciding againft the immediate interefts of the French Monarch.

If it be faid that Mr. Eden has fecured to the inhabitants of this country as complete an exemption from the operation of the *Droit D'Aubaine*, as was obtained under the Treaty of *Utrecht* in the year 1713, (an affertion which is by no means to be maintained, but which is not worth the detail of a regular refutation) let it be remembered, that events have taken place fince that period, which ought to have made it peculiarly the duty of a negociator of the prefent day, to have demanded a plain, unambiguous, decifive arrangement upon the fubject.

I refer the reader to a narrative in my Appendix, which may prove interefting to him as an event of modern politics not generally known, and cannot fail to have a decifive influence upon his judgment, in convincing him of the abfolute neceffity which exifts for a clear and unequivocal underftanding between the two countries, as to the operation of this celebrated privilege.

He

He will there perceive of what miferable fubterfuges the French tribunals will avail themfelves, when deciding upon the operation of engagemenis that militate againft the immediate pecuniary interefts of their fovereign. If Mr. Eden knew of this inftance, he was guilty of a total defertion of his duty as a negociator, ftipulating for the perfonal privileges of his countrymen, not to have infifted upon the entire removal of an ambiguity, which experience had proved fo effentially to interfere with them;—if he did not, he was hardly fufficiently fkilled in the modern hiftory between the two countries, for an advantageous execution of the important duty he had affumed.

CORPORATE RIGHTS.

It would be unpardonable in a general inveftigation of this fort, to omit a detailed mention of fo alarming an innovation as that which is produced by the operation of this part of the Treaty. There are fome men whofe very conviction of the magnitude of the danger in this cafe, has inclined them to refift an opinion of its being really deducible

from

from the spirit of the Treaty itself; and there
are others who are difposed to difmifs the fubject negligently, as being too immediately de-
monftrative to require the formality of a regular enquiry.

Thofe who confider the extent of the injuries
refulting from this commercial fyftem as a pre-
fumption in favour of the negociator of it, muft
think very highly of him indeed; and if I
could be induced to look upon that as a de-
fenfible ground of partiality, I fhould unite
cordially in their good opinion. This is a novelty in defence, however, which I am not
entirely difpofed to acquiefce in; and am
equally averfe to a carelefs refignation of a
great point, merely becaufe much ingenuity
may not be demanded in the difcuffion of it.
I would rather be expofed to the imputation
of tedioufnefs in the way of over folicitude,
than be cenfured for a culpable neglect.

The Charter of the city of London, which
was held of confequence enough, to be ex-
preffly confirmed, even by Magna Charta itfelf, and afterwards by a particular act of the
legiflature (in 2. W. and M. c. 8.) has expli-
citly ftipulated, That no perfon fhall be per-

2   mitted

mitted to expose Goods to Sale in Shops, as artifts or retail dealers of any denomination except fuch perfon fhall firft have been admitted a Freeman of the faid Corporation, by fervice, birth-right, or redemption.

The precife terms, in which this invaluable privilege has been hitherto fecured, are exactly thefe, " No perfon, not being a Freeman of London, fhall keep any fhop, or other place, to put to fale, by retail, any goods, or wares, or ufe any handicraft trade for hire, gain, or fale, within the city, upon penalty of forfeiting five pounds for every fuch offence."

Let us then enquire, what are the new privileges, in direct violation of this facred compact, conferred upon the inhabitants of France, by the prefent Treaty. The following extract is copied from the

FIFTH ARTICLE.

" The fubjects of each of their faid Majefties may have leave and licence to come with their fhips, as alfo with the merchandizes and goods on board the fame, the trade and im-

T   portation

portation whereof are not prohibited by the laws of either kingdom, and to enter into the countries, dominions, cities, ports, places, and rivers of either party, fituated in Europe, to refort thereto, and to remain and refide there, without any limitation; *alfo to hire houfes*, or to lodge with other perfons, and to buy all lawful kinds of merchandizes, where they think fit, either from the firft maker or the feller, or in any other manner, whether in the public market for the fale of merchandizes, or in fairs, or wherever fuch merchandizes are manufactured or fold. They may likewife *depofit and keep* in their magazines and warehoufes, *the merchandizes brought from other parts, and afterwards expofe the fame to fale,* without being in any wife obliged, unlefs willingly and of their own accord, to bring the faid merchandizes to the marts and fairs. Neither are they to be burthened with any impofitions or duties on account of the faid freedom of trade, or for any other caufe whatfoever, except thofe which are to be paid for their fhips and merchandizes conformably to the regulations of the prefent Treaty, or thofe to which the fubjects of the two contracting parties fhall themfelves be liable."

Left

Left, however, the privileges included in
the above extract should be suspected of having been conveyed in terms of less clearness
and precision, than suited the wishes and interests of at least one of the contracting parties, Mr. Eden has consented to go a step further; and to confirm the inhabitants of the rival empire in the possession of these new
rights, in words as unambiguous as the effect
of them is destructive and unconstitutional.
He adds, " and they shall have right to re-
move themselves, as also their wives, children,
and servants, together with their merchandi-
dizes, property, goods or effects, whether
bought or imported, wherever they shall think
fit, out of either kingdom, by land and by
sea, on the rivers and fresh water; after dif-
charging the usual duties, *any law; privilege,
grant, immunities,* or *customs,* to the contrary
thereof in any wise notwithstanding."

Now, to what in the preceding passages,
can the term *immunity* have any possible application ? Not to the removal of the citizens,
their wives, &c. because that being hitherto
a penal prohibition, would have been revoked
by a repeal of the statute enjoining it, and
not by the grant of an *immunity.*

T 2   To

CORPORATE RIGHTS.

To what elfe, then, in thefe quoted paffages
can it extend?—To nothing, clearly, but to
the privileges contained in the firft extract, au-
thorifing the future eftablifhment of French
fhops in the metropolis; for nothing elfe is expreffed in this part of the article, to which,
by any conftruction of fenfe, or grammatical
arrangement it can have the fmalleft reference.
The fact indeed is, that in all legal accep-
tation, the term immunity fignifies not the do-
nation of a privilege, but fpecifically the exemption from a cuftom or duty; and in this
fignification it is accurately employed by Mr.
Eden, when he informs us, as by the refult
of this article, we are to our coft informed,
that in difregard of paft ufage, in contempt of
any pre-eftablifhed cuftom, in defiance of exifting charters, Frenchmen, from the date of
the prefent treaty, are legitimate freemen of
the city of London, without the labour of ap-
prenticefhip, or expence of purchafe, and
are entitled to a full and equal participation
of their beft and deareft privileges.

It may perhaps be fuggefted to this, that in
the conduct of a great ftate meafure, exten-
tenfive in its fubject, and complex in its ar
-rangement

rangement, a cafual inaccuracy of expreffion,
(for fuch, to be defended, this muft be maintained to be) is not much to be infifted upon.
How far this explanation will be accepted by
Mr. Eden, a gentleman at leaft as converfant
in the meaning of words, as experienced in
the arts of political negociation, it is not for
us to determine.—Whether he has a juft right,
however, to avail himfelf, even of this ami-
cable fubterfuge, will be beft feen by an attention to the following confideration:

Mr. Eden, in the formation of the treaty of
which we fpeak, and for the fuccefsful adjuftment of which, he is to receive the future
rewards of his country, has made it an almoft
undeviating principle with himfelf to tranf-
cribe accurately and implicitly from the
Treaty of Utrecht, in the year 1713.—
The queftion then arifes, does the Treaty
of Utrecht contain any claufe of the kind
and tendency now complained of? —— Is
there any thing in it that can have the effect
of admitting French citizens into a full participation of the advantages and privileges of
the citizens of London? To this we anfwer
NO, not a word. Is there any thing in it on
the

the contrary, that goes to the pofitive inter-diction of any fuch participation? To this we anfwer YES; and that in terms as direct and intelligibly pointed to the prefervation of Britifh rights, as Mr. Eden's are ftrong and explicit in the violation of them. In the fifth article of the Treaty of Utrecht; which correfponds with the fifth article in the treaty of Mr. Eden, after having admitted, as is alfo done in the modern counterpart of it, that the fubjects of the two countries may be reci-procally permitted to refort to the cities, ports, &c. of the refpective kingdoms, and to lay up, and keep in their magazines, and warehoufes, all kinds of lawful merchandizes; we find thefe exprefs words, " on this condi-tion, however, *that they fhall not fell the fame by retail in fhops, or any where elfe.*" Can there be found in the Englifh language, terms more direct, and unequivocal? Did Mr. Eden de-viate then from fo intelligible a precedent, by mere accident or inattention? Did he intro-duce words deftructive to the very effence of his avowed original, and abrogatory of its moft important prohibitions without a purpofe or defign? If there be a man fo devoted to a blind and dangerous credulity, fo abandoned

to

to the purpofes of a particular party, as to believe this, we muft refign him to the quiet poffeffion of opinions, that are evidently not to be ftirred by fact, or fhaken by the plaineft deductions of reafon.

Two points in this extraordinary tranfaction are eftablifhed, beyond all power of controverfy. That by the terms of Mr. Eden's treaty, the boafted exclufion claimed under the Chartered Rights of the City of London, is abrogated and deftroyed.

That by the terms of the Treaty of Utrecht, which in all other cafes, he has copied with fo fervile, and obedient an accuracy, thofe revered privileges are left, as every Englifhman muft wifh them for ever to have remained, facred and fecure.

We have two reafons, therefore for believing, that the claufe complained of, was voluntarily introduced, and deliberately intended to bear the interpretation now imputed to it. Firft, That we find the actual terms of it calculated to convey no meaning at all; if not that, which we annex to it. Secondly, That we we find the exprefs, and fpecific reverfe of this meaning in the acknowledged precedent from which it was tranfcribed, in every other part. By avoiding to adopt words, that were obtruded upon his obfervation, which he could not avoid attending to, and by which, (if adopted) the corporate rights of his countrymen would have been completely fecured, we can be at no lofs to determine, what could be his real and deliberate intention, when he made ufe of language, the obvious meaning, and literal conftruction of which, goes directly to the in-invafion of thofe fame privileges.—Is it at all neceffary to enlarge on fo evident a principle?—In the whole progrefs and conduct of this Treaty, Mr. Eden had affumed one uniform line of proceeding, from which he has never fubftantially deviated; that where it was the intention of the parties to introduce the fame regulation into the modern treaty which exifted previoufly in that of Utrecht, he has not only adopted the regulation itfelf, but the words alfo in which it was conveyed. If it had been his intention then to imitate the virtuous rejection of this dangerous innovation, which he found in the precedent before him; why did he not, in conformity to his conftant ufage,

usage, imitate also the terms in which that intention was expressed ?—But the reverse of this
was the new principle that he and his coadju-
tors in office meditated to establish, and they
have accordingly made use of language most
clearly and unequivocally calculated to ex-
press their meaning. Our judgments are
equally satisfied in this case, from the words
which Mr. Eden has avoided to use, and those
which he has used. We are equally convinced
from both, that the real, true, and systematic
purpose of himself, and the other members of
the Cabinet, with whom he co-operated in the
arrangement of this important negociation, was
directly and unambiguously this :---" To admit all the subjects of France, without excep-
tion or distinction into a full, free, and indis-
criminate participation of all the privileges
of the City of London, which have been hitherto deemed exclusively their own, under
the claim and sanction of their charter."

What has been said of the charter of the city
of London, is equally applicable to all the
other corporate bodies in the kingdom.

To extend this consideration a little further :

U   Though

Though any Englifhman may fet up a fhop in any town which is not a corporate town, yet, as the law now ftands, no foreigner can do fo. He may hire a houfe, it is true, but he is cir-cumfcribed in the ufe to which he fhall appro-priate it—for habitation is the exprefs limita-tion put on it by Blackftone, p. 372, vol. 1.— By 32 Hen. VIII. c. 16. § 13. No alien can take any fhop, under a penalty of 5 *l*.—nor can any one let a fhop to an alien under the fame penalty.

Thus, not only corporate bodies have been hitherto fecured in the exclufive poffeffion of their internal trade, in the way of retail, by the operation of their particular charter ; but by this ftatute an equal privilege has been enjoyed by every other town in the kingdom.

It has been faid, that Blackftone himfelf has expreffed an opinion, that the ftatute allud-ed to has been in effect fuperceded by the re-gulations of pofterior laws.—This is an evi-dent mifconception of his meaning—He fays, indeed, that the 5th Eliz. c. 7. virtually re-pealed thofe ftatutes of Henry VIII. which prohibited alien artificers from working for themfelves, or otherwife than as fervants to
Englifhmen,

Englishmen; but there is no pretence for saying that it repealed the penalties upon taking
shops.

But what puts the matter out of all doubt
is, that many actions have been brought
upon that statute, long since the statute of
Elizabeth, which are collected and abridged
even in every Law Dictionary; and to them
I refer the reader who may be desirous of
pursuing this important subject to its last stage
of precision:

'I shall only subjoin, by way of anticipated
reply to those who may be of opinion, that
it cannot be the intention of the present
treaty to dissolve these corporate rights, because they are so demonstratively protected by
the direct law of the land; that there is a
sweeping clause towards the conclusion of
the treaty, which stipulates that the King of
England shall endeavour to prevail with his
Parliament to rescind all such laws as may
impede the due execution of any of the agree-
ments contained in it.—Some laws therefore
were known to be infringed—and why not these
among the number ?—If it be suggested, that
though all this be admitted, yet that the right

U 2   between

between the two countries is reciprocal, I
fhall leave it to the fenfe and feeling of my
fellow-citizens to determine, how far an obvious inducement to emigration is to be confidered. as an adequate compenfation for the participation of their retail market with the inhabitants of the rival kingdom.

The PRINCIPLE of FREE BOTTOMS making FREE GOODS.

The   article contains the admiffion
of this long-refifted principle on the part of
England; but as the fact is not attempted to
be denied, that the right fo frequently claimed
by other powers, and fo perfeveringly oppofed
by us, is now conceded fully and unequivocally, there is no particular neceffity for quot-
ing the exprefs words of the treaty, nor of ar-
guing upon their conftruction.

I feel myfelf relieved from all neceffity of
reforting to any perfonal argument on this fubject, by an appeal to the opinion of a writer,
who, whatever may be his other claims to the
favour or difefteem of his country, has unquef-
tionably contended this point with equal information

formation and ability. I mean Mr. *Charles Jenkinson*, who, in a pamphlet publifhed by him, in the year 1757, entitled " A Difcourfe on the Conduct of Great Britain, in Refpect to Neutral Nations," has moft completely eftablifhed the impolicy and injuftice of this celebrated claim, and the almoft unremitting pertinacity of Great Britain in refufing the admiffion of it.

I can advance nothing that would be in any degree either fo entertaining or fo inftructing as *Mr. Jenkinfon's* authority, upon this fubject, and therefore I fhall quote a paffage from his book, which appears to me to contain the moft decifive and unanfwerable objection to this part of the treaty.

" Let us now look on what has been faid;
" the deduction which I have made, hath I
" fear been tedious, but the importance of
" the fubject of force led me into it. I flatter
" myfelf however that it has appeared, that
" reafon, authority, and practice, all join to
" fupport the caufe I defend. By reafon, I
" have endeavoured to trace out thofe princi-
" ples on which this right of capture is ground-

4   " ed,

" ed, and to give that weight to my own fenti-
" ments, which of themfelves they would not
" deferve, I had added the authorities of the
" ableft writers on this fubject; and laftly, I
" have entered largely into the conduct of
" nations, that I might not only lay thereby a
" broader foundation for this right, but that I
" might the more fully illuftrate, by the ex-
" travagant pretenfions of other ftates in this
" refpect, the prefent moderation of England;
" no age or country ever gave a greater extent
" to the commerce of neutral nations, and we
" have feen, that moft in the fame circum-
" ftances have confined it within much naf-
" rower bounds.

" The liberty of navigation in fair con-
" ftruction can mean no more than the right
" of carrying to any port unmolefted, the pro-
" duce of one's own country or labour, and
" bringing back the emoluments of it. But
" can it be lawful, that you fhould extend
" this right to my detriment, and when it
" was meant only for your advantage, that you
" fhould exert it in the caufe of my enemy?
" Each man hath a right to perform certain
" actions, but if the deftruction of another
" fhould follow from them, would not this be
" a juft

" a juft reafon of reftraint?—The rights of
" mankind admit of different degrees, and
" whenever two of thefe come into competi-
" tion, the loweft in the fcale muft always
" give place to the higher.—But.you will fay,
" that you have a profit in doing this; if, how-
" ever, it is otherwife unjuft, will that confi-
" deration convert it into a right?—If you
" mean, that your own commerce ought to be
" free, that right is not in the leaft denied
" you; but if under this difguife you intend
" to convey freedom to the commerce of the
" enemy, what policy or what juftice can re-
" quire it? What can neutral nations defire
" more than to remain amidft the ravages of
" war in the fame happy circumftances which
" the tranquility of peace would have afforded
" them? But can any right from hence arife
" that you fhould take occafion of the war
" itfelf to conftitute a new fpecies of traffick,
" which in peace you never enjoyed, and which
" the neceffity of one party is obliged to grant
" you, to the detriment, perhaps the deftruc-
" tion, of the other?—If this right was ad-
" mitted, it would become the intereft of all
" commercial ftates to promote diffention
" among their neighbours; the quarrels of
" others would be a harveft to themfelves,
" and

" and from the contentions of others they
" would gather wealth and power."

Having at an eafy expence fatisfied the mind
of my reader, of the danger and injuftice attending the admiffion of this right, (or if he
retains a doubt on the fubject, having no expedient for removing it nearly fo efficacious as
a reference to the equally irrefiftable arguments
contained in the whole of Mr. Jenkinfon's
pamphlet) I find myfelf in fairnefs compelled
to paufe here, and to refift with all the energy
of truth, contending on the fide of innocence,
an obloquy which has gone abroad with refpect to Mr. Jenkinfon, that he was the ad-
vifer or fabricator of the prefent treaty.—This
is amongft the idle rumours which difgrace
political attachments.—Here you behold an
inftance where zeal outftrips information, and
where the regard for a party fubdues the fuperior obligation which belongs to candour.
In thefe violences I have no fympathy—let me
avoid, therefore, the reproach of them.

Is it to be believed, that a man bearing a
high lead in the political goverment of the
ftate in which he lives, claiming, and having
received the diftinguifhed renumerations which
a demo-

a democratic conftitution laudably extends to
prefumed virtue, or to attefted induftry, where-
ever found, or in whatever fhape of original
depreffion they prefent themfelves, that he
fhould take a part in the forniation of a great
national contract ; that he fhould bind the
country to which he owes fuch obligation, to
the adoption of principles which he himfelf has
proved beyond controverfy, inequitable, and
out of all queftion injurious, and even vitally
dangerous, is a fuppofition of monftrous and
unprecedented depravity, which will not be believed even of the torturous politics of Mr.
Jenkinfon, but on much better authority than
that which at prefent fuftains it.—Let the
reader examine the prefent treaty, and confult
Mr. Jenkinfon's pamphlet, and then let him
be afked, if both be the fabrication of one
hand, why the author of both was made a
peer ? Was it for uniform talents, or for con-
fiftency of uniform principle ?—My anfwer is,
the whole report is a calumny, and that he
was totally without any participation in the
difgraceful tranfaction of the prefent treaty.—
Mr. J. proves farther, (to ufe his own words)
" That the laws of France univerfally contra-
" dict her treaties ; and that it was wife in
" her to eftablifh it as a general maxim of na-
" tional law among other countries, and that

X   " expe-

" experience had proved to her the ufe of it " in time of war." Let Englifhmen think of this, and determine the propriety of Great Britain's eftablifhing this principle*.

It cannot but be apparent to the reader, that independent of the immediate difadvantages which refult from this treaty to diftinct and fpecific interefts, there may be others which, though lefs practicable to be claffed under any particular denomination, yet in their nature are not therefore of lefs confequence to the community.—Of each of thefe I fhall proceedto fay a few words, with a brevity injurious to the importance of the fubject, but demanded from me by the almoft unavoidable length to which this difcuffion has already extended.

It is to be obferved, then, that though it fhould be admitted, in direct contradiction to the internal evidence of the cafe, that the prefent *ad valorem* duties are not in an *equal degree* a protection to the feveral branches of the mutual trade affected by the treaty, but that England is in a ftate of decided advantage, refulting from the fuperiority of her fkill, yet it is clear, that the moment (and no one can pretend that fuch a period may not fome time or another arrive) that France attains an equa-

* Vide the Collection of Treaties, publifhed by Debrett.

lity

lity to us in the make of her manufactures,
from that period there is an end to all pretence
of reciprocity in the Treaty. Becaufe in all
articles of manufacture both Countries will
then ftand in a fituation of fimilar advantage,
and France will have the exportation of her
wines and brandies into England, for which we
have no articles of native produce to reciprocate a balance in return.

That our trade with Spain and Portugal
was carried on folely in Britifh fhipping, which
from the fuperior cheapnefs of French freightage, cannot poffibly in the very fame articles,
continue to be the cafe in future.

That even the fmuggling between the two
countries will be hereafter conducted in French
veffels, a circumftance hitherto new and more
mifchievous in its confequences than fome
readers may be inclined to fuppofe it. There
was this wretched folace even in the illegiti-
mate traffick of this country, that if it injured
the honeft and direct trader, yet it involved in
it a fource of ftrength to our marine, an advantage no longer probable to refult from it,
though the practice itfelf be likely to prevail
to a much larger, and certainly not lefs injurious extent.

X 2

That

That we have chofen the hour of weaknefs
and depreffion for the introduction of innovations, ruinous 'to the finance, and therefore
alarming to the credit of the country,—at leaft
dangerous to our commerce, and unafcertain-
able as to the extent of their influence upon' our
general policy.

That we have totally deprived ourfelves of
the poffible faculty of making a fingle friend of
any fort of confequence amongft all the States
of Europe, becaufe by ftipulating to extend
every favourable conceffion to France, which
we may agree to beftow upon any other power,
we can retain nothing in our power to give,
which it can be at all worth their while to ac-
cept.

That we have treated Ireland in this new
fyftem, in fome inftance with an illiberal and
unfifterly neglect, and in others with an undif-
tinguifhing and reprehenfible indulgence.——
Sometimes fhe is ufed with the weak fondnefs
of a fpoilt child, and at others with unnatu-
ral rigour, as if fhe were an alien to our blood.
We enable her to annihilate our manufactures
of iron, which are effential to us, and comparatively indifferent to her, and abfolutely-fhut up
her exportation of linen which we cannot
make,

make, and which is above all points of trade the which is not only moſt congenial to Ireland, but that in which ſhe moſt excels.

That the inhabitants of France are much more likely, from various cauſes not neceſſary here to enumerate, to incur large debts in England, than the inhabitants of this country in that.

That by the general conſtitution of the French Courts of Judicature, and by the particular embarraſſments reſulting from certain recent edicts, it is difficult almoſt to a degree of impracticability, for a foreigner of any denomination, to recover a debt there through the medium of any legal proceſs.

That by an *Arret*, the French King can difſolve the obligations of juſtice, and not only releaſe his ſubjects from the neceſſity of paying their debts, but make it even penal ſo to do.

That the operations of the law of England are ſteady and uniform,—unyielding to influence,—unbending to authority,—not to be impeded even by the powerful temptation of political advantage, but diſpenſing equal juſtice to the ſubjects of all countries.

That

That if a war therefore fhould take place between France and England, and furely it is not yet the fafhion to deprecate the poffibility of fuch a contingency, the former will have to affift them in the commencement of their hoftility, the whole of that part of our capital which is invefted in their hands, under the defcription of debts, while England muft difcharge her demands to them to the uttermoft exactnefs.

That in paft wars with France and with Spain, our European commerce was but little interrupted, as we could ftill fupply the Portuguefe, and through their medium had the avenues preferved to us to Spain.

That by the treaty of Friendly Alliance formed between France, Spain, and Portugal, fo late as the year 1783, aided by the co-operation of the injuries offered to the latter power by the ftipulations of the prefent treaty, Portugal is always likely in future to confpire in the views of France, and to be a party in her hoftilities.

That by this means, a war with France will not only involve in it a total annihilation of our invaluable trade with Spain and Portugal; but not leave us a fingle port from the

the *Baltic* to *St. Helena,* in which our ſhip-
ping can take refuge either from the enemy
or from diſtreſs.

But, above all, let it adhere about the minds
of Engliſhmen, and ſink deep in their hours
of ſerious reflection, that after effect ſhall be
given to the preſent treaty, almoſt the whole
of our European commerce will be confined to
ONE CHANNEL.—If a war ſhould ariſe, therefore, we ſhall have that to accompliſh in a moment of diſtraction, alarm, and confuſion,
which is always difficult in times of the moſt
compoſed tranquility, to diſcover new avenues
for our trade, and new reſources for our revenue.

I promiſed to the reader on this part of my
undertaking, that I ſhould not preſume ſo far
on the liberality of a patience which I muſt
already have expoſed to a ſufficient trial as to
purſue the great ſubjects which I have here
juſt touched upon, through all the detail of
elaborate enquiry which ſo juſtly belongs to
them—I ſhall leave it to the richer ſoil of his
own mind, to mature theſe embryo ſketches
to the ſize and vigour which, with the leaſt
culture, they cannot fail to attain, content
and

2

and happy, if, after much labour, much dry
calculation, and much confultation of unen-
tertaining, but authentic and neceffary docu-
ment, I fhall have fucceeded in faving one
branch of manufacture, or one point of the
perfonal privileges of my countrymen from
the devaftation of a meafure which I fincerely
look upon as uniting all the poffible deprava-
tions of the human intellect,—as having been
conceived in Madnefs, born in Folly, and fent
out into the world in Ignorance !

F I N I S.

APPENDIX.

APPENDIX.

Nº 1

Memorial of Charles Howard, (afterwards Duke of Norfolk,) Esq. of Greystock, and Miss Frances Howard, of the family of Norfolk, in England; presented to the British ambassador at Paris, concerning a claim of theirs to the effects of a relation who died in France. Translated from the French.

MR. and Miss Howard, and with them all the English nation, do, by the good offices of the ambassador, claim the execution of the XIIIth Article of the Treaty of Utrecht, and of the declaration of 1739, by both which the subjects of Great Britain are allowed to succeed to the personal estates of their relations deceased in France; in the same manner as the subjects of the most Christian King are authorised to inherit the like estates of their relations dying in England.

Y   These

Thefe laws have been executed in this particular, with the utmoft exactnefs on the part of the Englifh.

They can bring the moft authentic proofs, and are are able to maintain by a number of examples, which have happened even during the late war, that this execution has been totally in favour of the French; infomuch, that even when there was no precife law upon this point, the ufage alone, which was practifed in England, was fufficient to give this nation a right to exact from France a reciprocality which is founded on the right of nature and nations. It is by the favour of thefe different titles, that Mr. and Mifs Howard prefume to demand their part of a fucceffion to the perfonal eftate of their uncle, who died in France : and yet the Judges of the Chatelet, before whom their claim was at firft carried, have not judged proper to admit it ; and their fentence has been confirmed by an arret.

It was difficult to conceive what could be the motives for fuch fingular decifions; efpecially if it be confidered, that the fucceffion in queftion was open before the late war.

Mr.

Mr. and Mifs Howard were in England at
the time they received the news, by a letter
from their attorney. If they can believe this
letter, the judges were determined against
them for two powerful reasons, which were
propofed by the King's advocate to the Chatelet: the one, that the treaty of Utrecht, on
which they founded their claim, had not been
regiftered in parliament: the other, that the
argument does not hold good, of the French
being admitted to fucceed to the personal
eftates of their relations who die in England;
becaufe that admiffion is not founded, fay
they, on the treaty of Utrecht, but on the
conftitution of that kingdom, which admits
to that kind of fucceffion other foreigners,
equally with French; whereas, according to
the conftitution of France, they cannot be allowed there but by virtue of a naturalization,
or of a particular treaty, duly regiftered.

Although this was fufficiently refuted by
the words of the treaty of Utrecht, and the
declaration of 1739, which makes no diftinction in the reputed quality of relations, according to which they ought to fucceed; never-
thelfs, to fet it more effectually afide, the late
Mr. Simon de Mofart, who was charged with

the

the defence of Mr. and Miſs Howard, thought proper to have it confulted in England, in or-der to know what was the cuſtom there in this caſe. The caſe was at firſt ſtated in this man-ner :

If an Engliſhman born happens to die in England, without children, and inteſtate, and having relations born, and always reſiding in France, it is aſked, Will they be intitled to partake the ſucceſſion to the perſonal eſtate of the defunct, equally with his relations in the ſame degree of kindred, born and educated in England ?

The anſwer given to this queſtion was con-ceived in the following manner :

The Council having confidered, is of opi-nion, that in confequence of the ſtatutes of dif-tribution, the relations born in France have the ſame right to perſonal eſtates as thoſe born in England.

This anſwer not having entirely ſatisfied the French advocate, in that it only ſpoke of the Statute of Diſtribution, and not of the Treaty of Utrecht, the execution of which was the
principal

principal debate in this caufe; he refumed the enquiry, and defired that the Englifh Council would give his opinion upon the following queftion: it is afked,

How do they in England underftand and execute the XIIIth article of the treaty of Utrecht? and if, in confequence of this treaty, a Frenchman living in France, could fucceed to an Englifhman, his relation, dying in England, being equally related with the Englifh heirs of the deceafed refiding in England? and what are the reafons upon which the Englifh ground their admiffion of the Frenchman to fucceed with the others?

The following is the next anfwer, which was fent from England.

The ufage of England is exactly agreeable to the XIIIth article of the treaty of Utrecht; the French relations being admitted to fucceed, equally with Englifh relations in the fame degree of kindred, to the perfonal eftate of an inteftate dying in England. The law of England does not, in this refpect, make any diftinction between foreigners and natural-born fubjects, and is conformed to the conftitution

tution of the Emperor Frederic II. tit. 1. fect. 10. and is founded as well on natural juftice, as commercial reafons. ..

It is to be obferved, that this clear and exprefs opinion is figned by the lord chief juftice of England, by the King's advocate and attorney-general, and confequently that it has all the marks of authority that any one can defire in matters of this kind.

In fhort, independently of the proofs which refulted from thefe pieces, Mr. and Mifs Howard offered farther to juftify, by the regifters of the courts of juftice in England, a crowd of examples of fucceffions of perfonal eftates, which have been recovered by French people of their Englifh relations. They cited, among others, that of Mrs. Cantillon, a French woman, actually refiding at the Nouvelles Catholiques, in Paris, who having claimed, during the laft war, the perfonal eftate of Mr. John Cantillon, her nephew, who died in Ireland, in 1754, being a captain in one of his Britannic Majefty's regiments, was put into poffeffion of the effects of this fucceffion, by the Court of Doctors Commons, to the prejudice of his other relations; and fhe has received

3   ceived

ceived, in confequence, 650 l. fterling, and
the remainder to be remitted to her imme-.
diately.

So many proofs accumulated, left no re-
fource for the pretended argument of incapacity, which they had at firft oppofed to
Mr. and Mifs Howard : they waited. patiently
the fuccefs of their demand, till they underftood, with an extreme furprife, that it had
been rejected by a. fentence of the Chatelet.
And.the. affair being afterwards carried before
Parliament, an arret was paffed, which confirmed that fentence.

THE END.

ERRATA in the following Pages.

Page 18—Instead of Cottons might have been sent *to* this Country, read, *from* this Country.

P. 36—Instead of, it would have been idle in *her* to have asked in *us*, and us to have granted, read, and in *us* to have granted, &c.

P. 45—Instead of, French Woollens, till lately laid under prohibitory duties, read, *were* till lately, &c.

P. 80—Instead of, she has besides many of Dying Drugs, read, many Dying Drugs.

P. 89—Instead of, to have satisfied the most systematic parliament, read, the most systematic cruelty.

P. 148—Instead of the —— Article contains, &c. read, the 20th Article contains, &c.

P. 73—From the same iron in the 8th line, add, for the French market.

P. 91—Instead of 25 per cent. read, 24.

P. 96—Makes a difference in price to markets, dele to markets.

P. 130—For smugglers, read, smuggler.

P. 124—For 5s. read, 5d.

893 .6